ALSO BY DUSTIN GRINNELL

Fiction

The Genius Dilemma
Without Limits
The Empathy Academy
The Healing Book

Nonfiction

Lost & Found
The Velvet Ghetto

BEDRIDDEN

A Novella

DUSTIN GRINNELL

BEDRIDDEN
A University of California Health Humanities Press
Trade Paperback Book

An Imprint of The Virtuoso Press

Cover Design by Dustin Grinnell

Editorial Offices:
Humanities & Social Sciences
490 Illinois Street, Floor 7
San Francisco, CA 94143-0850

ISBN (print): 979-8-9926888-7-0

Printed in USA

As is often the case in my writing, the central idea of this novel-la—the Nietzschean notion that pain and suffering can be transformative—emerged from personal experience. In 2015, after moving to California, I began to experience mysterious physical symptoms, ranging from back pain and aching joints to tingling limbs and headaches. When doctors couldn't explain them, I went on a personal quest for answers.

I consulted everyone from physical therapists to psychiatrists, exploring both the body and the mind. Along the way, I faced not only chronic pain but buried emotions. What started as a search for physical healing turned into something deeper: an emotional journey through crisis, self-discovery, and ultimately, post-traumatic growth.

After extensive therapy, reading books and writing essays, I came to understand that a problem of the mind was manifesting physically in my body. In short, I was dealing with a psychosomatic illness, in which psychological stress and suppressed emotions, like grief, anger and sadness, show up as physical symptoms. Understanding this and recovering from it triggered a period of personal growth for me. While the experience was scary and unsettling at the time, it left me humbler and more emotionally open.

It also led to a dark fascination with the shift in consciousness that mental or physical illness can bring about in some people. In my reading, I discovered how other people have emerged from such episodes transformed. Carl Jung, for example, went through a psychological crisis after breaking with Freud in 1913. During his "confrontation with the unconscious," Jung explored his dreams and fantasies in seclusion, eventually producing some of his most important contributions to psychology: the collective unconscious, archetypes, and individuation. Such experiences have been known by different names—post-traumatic growth, psychological renewal, spiritual awakening—but each has led the sufferer to a deeper understanding of themselves or the world.

Knowing this, I couldn't help but wonder: What if someone craved a breakthrough so desperately, they were willing to make themselves sick to achieve it? I explore that idea in this book, in which a psychiatrist undergoes his own "breakdown-to-breakthrough" experience—far more exaggerated than my own—and meets someone who persuades him to try manufacturing illness in order to derive its perceived benefits.

I found a model for the clinic in the story in conversation with my friend Ellen, whose interest in illness stemmed from a tick bite and the ensuing chronic Lyme disease that upended her life. Her illness journey had led her to pursue a PhD in anthropology, specifically folklore, and to write her dissertation on the Adirondack Cottage Sanitarium, a New York institution founded in the mid-1880s for patients with tuberculosis (TB).

Given my brush with psychosomatic illness and my interest in stories of healing, I urged Ellen to tell me more, and she regaled me with tales of Dr. Edward Livingston Trudeau, the founder of the sanatorium. While gravely ill with TB, Trudeau left New York City in 1873 for the Adirondack Mountains in upstate New York. When his health unexpectedly improved, he credited the fresh mountain air and built a home in the tiny settlement of Saranac Lake.

In 1884, Trudeau founded the Adirondack Cottage Sanitarium— nicknamed "the San"—for early-stage TB patients, with a model of care that emphasized rest, fresh air, hygiene, nutrition, and optimism. The institution grew to over fifty buildings, including many small, four-patient "cure cottages," and treated around four hundred patients a year, though many more came to the village "chasing a cure." By the turn of the century, Saranac Lake had become a world-famous health resort and a center for medical research.

Intending to learn more about this historic healing center, I made the five-hour drive from Boston to Saranac Lake, where calm lakes mirrored pine-covered hills and brightly painted Victorian homes. I wandered through the charming downtown, past old brick buildings, and made my way to the Saranac Laboratory Museum, where I read about patients from all walks of life who had come to this place in hopes of recovery.

When I got back from my trip, I invited Ellen onto my podcast, *Curiously*, where we talked about her dissertation and what made the Adirondack Cottage Sanitarium so special. She had interviewed dozens of former patients for her dissertation, and one insight struck us both: Many said their time at the sanatorium was among the best of their lives, a phrase that came up repeatedly in her doctoral research. These were people battling a deadly illness, many of whom didn't survive, so how could that time possibly have been the best of their lives?

One key to understanding this lies in the simplicity of their daily routines: meals, recreation, and treatments all followed a strict schedule, relieving many of the everyday burdens people usually face. Ellen also touched on the fact that Dr. Trudeau's sanatorium provided not only structure, good nutrition, fresh air, and rest but something more elusive: community.

Every day, doctors and nurses would wheel patients onto wraparound "cure porches" to breathe in the mountain air, chat with fellow patients, build friendships, and even fall in love. One former patient, writing under the pen name Dorothy Palmer Hines, based her first novel, *No Wind of Healing*, on her time at the sanatorium. She noted that many patients felt united by a common purpose: "This was a strange land where people drawn from all ways of life were all leveled then by the common bond—the search for health and the desire to shed despair."

Before you get to the story, I'd be remiss if I didn't offer a brief disclaimer. While my own illness journey led to post-traumatic growth, this isn't true for everyone. This novella is a work of fiction and uses the literary form to explore ethical dilemmas rather than to advance a philosophy of illness as transformation. Each person's illness is unique, and not all of us recover with insights or breakthroughs. Suffering—sorry to say, Nietzsche—is not inherently ennobling or clarifying; at times it can distort judgment or foster obsession. Some, tragically, do not get better or recover. But for some—myself included, as well as Calvin Bloom—illness can be a source of knowledge and growth, even breakthrough.

Dustin Grinnell
Winthrop, Massachusetts
January 2026

In the spring of 2017, Dr. Calvin Bloom, a pioneering psychiatrist, founded the Bloom Center for Counseling Services with the goal of addressing deep psychological and emotional troubles using conventional psychotherapy alongside psychiatric treatments that went beyond mainstream approaches. His methods were rooted in the suffering he himself had undergone in his quest to heal the mentally sick.

During a yearlong struggle with psychosomatic illness, which you'll read about in the first few chapters of the enclosed book, Dr. Bloom came to believe that a period of illness could, under certain circumstances, stimulate a dramatic personality change. It wasn't until he met one particular patient, Kendall, that he established the radical healing program he'd become known for: Project Breakthrough.

The idea that forcing a person to become sick could promote a powerful positive change in their personality didn't sit well with me at first. It wasn't until I saw the now-defunct program through the evolutionary theory of punctuated equilibrium that I finally came around to its potential. Proposed in 1972 by Niles Eldredge and Stephen Jay Gould, the theory argues that some evolutionary changes don't occur gradually, but rather in intense, rapid spurts triggered by dramatic environmental pressure. It's my belief that that is how Project Breakthrough worked.

The following book is a literary account of Dr. Bloom's brush with psychosomatic illness, his founding of the Bloom Center and Project Breakthrough, and the events leading up his untimely death in 2019. A friend and mentor of his, I volunteered to compile his writings in hopes that others could perhaps benefit from his story and the insights contained within it.

I encourage you to read on with an open mind and suspend judgment. Try to understand where Dr. Bloom was coming from and what he was trying to accomplish through his work.

Arthur Pratt, MD
Martha's Vineyard, Massachusetts
June 2021

As for sickness, are we not almost tempted to ask whether we could get along without it?

—Frederick Nietzsche

Your vision will become clear only when you can look into your heart. Who looks outside, dreams; who looks inside, awakens.

—C.G. Jung

Out of suffering have emerged the strongest souls; the most massive characters are seared with scars.

—Kahlil Gibran

Chapter One

When I graduated from Harvard Medical School, most of my peers already knew what area of medicine they wanted to specialize in—neurology, anesthesiology, rheumatology. I didn't have a clue where I should focus.

I considered becoming a surgeon, liking the simplicity of fixing what was broken. However, whenever I examined a surgical case, I was always more concerned with how the patient had gotten sick in the first place than with what needed repairing.

Most doctors are like mechanics. If a car's brakes fail, a mechanic may replace the brake pads or rotors. But they won't explore the deeper causes of the brakes' failure. To them, it makes no difference whether the failure came from natural wear and tear or excessive damage due to the owner's driving patterns. To me, however, understanding the underlying causes of a problem are crucial to the final solution.

Early on in medical school, I became aware that not everyone shared this belief. One of my teachers responded to my desire to explore the deeper causes of conditions with a roll of his eyes. When I insisted that such knowledge could help us stop diseases before they started, he said our job as doctors was to diagnose and treat diseases, not prevent them.

Feeling alone in my views, I turned to writing to relieve my frustration. What began as stress relief soon became a passion. I began writing fictionalized accounts of patients I'd met on my rounds in the hospital. Eventually, anytime I worked with a patient, I'd daydream about how to use the experience in a story.

When some of my stories were published in medical humanities journals, I considered giving up medicine altogether and writing full-time. I had a talent for storytelling and a commercial mindset for selling stories to editors. I even derived great pleasure from the process of writing, looking forward to it each morning before I saw my patients. However, inventing stories for a living seemed like a precarious and financially risky existence.

Torn between choosing a specialty after graduating med school and focusing on writing, I ultimately decided to defer the start of my medical career for a year.

Hoping to reflect and find my way in life, I planned a long driving trip from Boston to California, thinking I'd rent a place in Southern California for a year or so while I wrote and published stories. In preparation for this trip, I stocked up on notebooks for writing, and packed most of my belongings away into storage so I could vacate my apartment.

As I prepared to notify my landlord of my impending departure, I began to second-guess my decision. I'd just graduated from the most prestigious medical school in the world, and now I was going to throw it all away to make up stuff on paper?

Moreover, I'd have to live on savings during the trip, and money was rather tight. Without a steady job, I'd also be forgoing health insurance. Questions swirled in my mind: Would I run out of money? Would I be able to cover a medical problem if there was an emergency? It would've been more practical to have just chosen a specialty that was close enough to my interests and figured things out while I had a job.

I decided to embarked on my adventure anyway.

A friend suggested I might be trying to escape my problems, but I believed the trip might help me gain better perspective on them. There's something about traveling—being on the move—that has always shaken up my life and increased my self-awareness. I was hoping to discover something about myself, something I needed to know. Perhaps when I returned from California, I'd have a new sense of balance and know what I wanted to do with my medical degree.

A day into my journey, somewhere in the middle of Pennsylvania, the physical symptoms began. They started in my fingers. I'd grab a metal doorknob and feel a sharp sting. The first few times it happened, I didn't think much of it, just pulled my hand from the knob and shook it until the feeling went away. I thought I might have a vitamin B deficiency, but even after supplementing with B vitamins, the stinging didn't go away.

A couple of days later, as I continued south, I took a trip to the bathroom and the toilet paper came away bright red when I wiped. I suspected hemorrhoids, so I bought hemorrhoidal wipes, thinking the issue would resolve itself over time. But the streaks of blood didn't stop, and I soon developed a sharp, cutting sensation in my rectum. I knew that meant I had an anal fissure, a special kind of misery. The pain grew so bad, I nearly cried with every bowel movement.

A week into my cross-country drive, tiny dark specks began to appear throughout my vision. These floaters, as they're called, were generally benign, but I was reminded of a patient I'd once seen who had fallen off his mountain bike and hit his head. The impact had shaken up the fluid in his eyes like flakes in a snow globe.

If the floaters had been my only symptom, I would've ignored them. Combined with the stinging in my fingers and the anal fissure, though, I couldn't shake the unsettling feeling that they might be signs of a more serious problem with my body.

Promising myself I'd make an appointment to see a doctor once I'd settled in California, I continued traveling. But my health only got worse from there.

A week and a half into the trip, in South Carolina, I woke up in the middle of the night in my hotel room gasping for air. Panicking, I struggled to focus on slowing my breathing and lowering my heart rate. After about twenty minutes, my mind was finally calm enough for me to return to sleep, but it was restless at best.

The next night, I woke up to find my right arm completely numb. Thinking I'd slept on it, I rolled onto my other side and tried to shake my arm to get the blood flowing. When I had to use my left hand to get my right arm to move, I had a moment of panic as I wondered if my arm was paralyzed. It was an alarming couple of minutes before sensation returned to my arm and I could move it again.

Once my arm was working and feeling all right, I brushed the incident off as a result of how I'd been sleeping and put it from my mind.

Days later, I was writing by hand in bed, where I did most of my writing, when the pen fell from my hand because my fingers had stopped working. When I didn't immediately regain control of them, I did what any person concerned about their health would do: I went to the emergency room.

The ER doctor examined me skeptically. "Are you experiencing high levels of stress?"

I shook my head and the doctor went on to order various tests. While I sat in the exam room and stared at the ceiling, I thought more about stress. I didn't feel stressed in the "fight or flight" sense, but the games my body was playing had worried me. I started to think about how important certainty had been in my life—knowing who I was and where I intended to go in my life. All of that had been replaced with uncertainty, destabilizing my sense of self.

The results of all the tests came back negative. No tumors, no lesions, no problems with my blood flow or neurocircuitry.

After reading off the results, the doctor scratched the back of his head. "Have you considered the possibility that you know too much?"

"What do you mean?"

"As a physician yourself, you know almost every possible way the body can go wrong. There was a time in med school when I became hypochondriacal, attributing sinister causes to any lump or bump. Maybe you're doing that here."

"No," I shot back. "This isn't psychosomatic. Something's wrong."

The doctor stood up. "Well, according to your blood work and imaging, everything is fine." He went on to suggest various ways to manage stress, like daily meditation and yoga.

I would've thought being told I was healthy would be a relief, but it wasn't. I wanted a diagnosis. Even if I were developing some terrible disease, at least then I'd know what was wrong and could take steps to try to get better.

Leaving the hospital disappointed, I got in my car and looked into the rearview mirror to adjust my wire-rimmed glasses. Pushing graying hair aside, I realized how haggard I looked.

I continued driving along the Eastern Seaboard until I reached Florida. That's when my body went haywire.

My fingers started tingling constantly. My stool contained more blood than ever. Every bowel movement produced such intense pain, I could barely sit for more than ten minutes at a time. My vision was clouded with dark specks. And my arm went numb with increasing frequency.

As I traveled through Florida, my symptoms progressed to a form of early-onset arthritis. My hands ached after writing for only a few hours. When I got out of bed, my lower back cracked and popped. By the time I hit Alabama, the symptoms felt more like fibromyalgia. My muscles hurt and my neck throbbed. Old injuries, like a strained Achilles tendon, resurfaced.

As my thoughts narrowed down to the pain and nothing else—not the weather, not a book I was trying to read—I became a hypochondriac. Hopes and desires became secondary concerns. I was now certain I was developing a catastrophic disease and the thought terrified me.

My biggest fear was that my immune system was turning on me. No one yet knows how an overactive immune system chooses the system it wages war on. If it chooses the nervous system, it'll cause multiple sclerosis. If it attacks insulin-producing cells in the pancreas, the result is Type 1 diabetes. Attacking the gastrointestinal tract leads to diseases like Crohn's disease, while targeting the joints causes rheumatoid arthritis.

Given that I had persistent back pain, I was most afraid of ankylosing spondylitis, a condition where inflammation causes the vertebrae in a person's back to fuse together.

No matter which autoimmune disease I might end up with, there was one thing I knew for certain: most of them had no cure. Steroids could control the out-of-control physiology, but that would only bring temporary relief.

It reached the point where no matter what I was doing, some part of my mind was always focused on what my immune system might be damaging at that very moment. What healthy tissues were my white blood cells looking to destroy today? No tissue or organ system was safe from an immune system in overdrive.

Chapter Two

One Sunday during my trip, I got a phone call from my grandmother, Edith, who for most of my adult life, called me on Sundays to check in. Usually, we'd chat about current events or med school, but this time was different. She heard the fear in my voice.

"What's wrong, Calvin? You sound nervous."

I told her I might be developing an autoimmune disease.

"Oh dear, I'm sorry," she replied. "Although I'm not entirely surprised."

"Why's that?"

"The Bloom family has a history of autoimmune conditions."

My face felt hot as a wave of anxiety surged through my body. Knowing I might have a genetic predisposition just made me more worried. But I wanted to know the details, so I urged her to tell me more.

"Your mom's sister has rheumatoid arthritis, and your dad's brother has Graves disease."

"What about you?"

"I seem to have gotten the worst of the bunch. For many years, I've had symptoms of multiple sclerosis, although the doctors have refused to call it MS."

I pressed for more details, but Edith seemed tired and didn't want to go into it.

"Do I have to worry about you, Cal?"

"Everything's fine, Gram. I'm sure my body will calm down once I get to California."

When I got off the phone, I was more scared than ever. And yet, I also felt motivated to find answers. It's one thing to have a vulnerability to an autoimmune disorder; it's another to manifest one. As a doctor, I'd met many patients who had genes for a certain health condition, but the disease didn't develop because of their lifestyle or other factors. Why had my immune system gone into high gear? I didn't think stress could be the answer, as the ER doctor had suggested. Instead, I searched for possible physical causes.

At first, I suspected a virus. A month before I left for my trip, I'd taken a week-long vacation in Costa Rica, where I'd gotten sick after eating a noodle dish. Had a viral infection triggered my symptoms?

I was halfway through my journey in West Texas when I decided to stop writing and focus all my time on trying to solve the mystery of my illness. I spent my nights in hotel rooms reading medical literature, researching my symptoms, and trying to match them to a disorder that I could take to a doctor as a diagnosis.

I grew neurotic and constant worry kept my body tight with tension. My neck, shoulders, and legs ached all the time. Occasionally, without any obvious trigger, my lower back would spasm, and I'd have to lie on the floor and stare at the ceiling until it subsided. To loosen my muscles, I soaked in Epsom salt baths, and I used my dwindling savings to get massages that only temporarily relieved my symptoms.

Hoping to solve the mystery that had taken over my life, I extended my stay in New Mexico by several days. I typed observations into my laptop or spoke them into a tape recorder while pacing my hotel room. I noted my symptoms on index cards and posted them on the walls. I drew arrows and lines between them, making connections in an attempt to develop some unified theory, but an elegant diagnosis eluded me.

Had I gone crazy? I didn't feel psychotic or that I'd broken from reality. I was just obsessed with figuring out what was going on with my body. Something must've started my symptoms, but I couldn't figure out the root cause. Was it a pathogen from something I'd eaten? A noxious chemical? A heavy metal, perhaps?

As I grew increasingly upset, I visited emergency rooms more and more. Each time, I brought in folders stuffed with articles and scientific papers. I showed the doctors flow charts to make the case that my immune system had turned on me.

Despite my tales of woe, the doctors pointed out that every test they ordered came back negative. I didn't have Lyme disease or an STD, and stool samples ruled out *Helicobacter pylori* and other viruses or bacteria. Imaging showed no lesions in my brain. There were no abnormal blood values, except for an elevated rheumatoid factor, which wasn't high enough to warrant a referral to a specialist.

Eventually, I grew paranoid that the doctors and nurses thought my symptoms were psychological or psychosomatic—that they believed it was all in my head. Sure, my behavior was a little crazy, but I was, without a doubt, experiencing real symptoms.

It wasn't until I was talking with my grandmother on the phone one Sunday that I began to consider what my doctors had been trying to get me to recognize: maybe I was suffering not from a disorder of the body, but from a disease of the mind.

Edith seemed willing to discuss her symptoms, which she believed were due to multiple sclerosis, so I asked how it all began. She told me that she'd enjoyed a successful career as an engineer before her health issues forced her into an early retirement. She explained how she'd worked in a toxic work environment that experienced rampant restructurings, fear of which made her deeply anxious. Her identity had been wrapped up in being an engineer, as she loved solving problems and took great pride in her work.

If she wasn't an engineer, who was she?

"After one particularly bad round of layoffs," she told me, "I began to experience numbness and tingling in my legs. I was sent to a neurologist, who conducted blood tests and imaging studies and found no signs of a neurological disease. But the symptoms got so bad, I was bound to a wheelchair."

"What did the doctors tell you?"

"I knew I was developing MS, but every doctor I met insisted I wasn't suffering from a physical disorder. Instead, I was likely dealing with a functional neurological disorder. Can you believe that, Calvin? They were telling me it was all in my head!"

I understood my grandmother's frustration. In medical school, I'd once tried to tell a patient that their tests suggested they were physiologically normal, their brain had no anatomical defects, and instead, the origin of their symptoms were psychogenic. The patient had resented being told that their symptoms weren't driven by a physical cause.

"What happened next?" I asked.

"I was referred to psychiatry, but I never followed up, too angry that my doctor thought I was a hypochondriac."

"Do you still believe you have multiple sclerosis?"

"I'm still in a wheelchair, aren't I?"

It was clear that Edith believed she had MS, despite her doctors telling her she didn't. Clearly, work stress had taken a physical toll on her body, and I wondered whether therapy might have helped her explore if her condition was influenced by emotions or unconscious conflicts.

At that moment, I started to think that I was dealing with the same problem my grandmother had been dealing with. My symptoms began with the start of my trip and intensified the farther I got from home and the sense of certainty I'd relied on.

Deciding to travel across the country and potentially write for a living, I'd ditched a future I'd been planning for over a decade. Ever since high school, I'd wanted to be a doctor and had looked forward to the day I carried that title and could help those in need. Now, though, I was floundering, trying to find my place in the world. Maybe my symptoms were driven by this major life change and the worry it caused.

I was in a hotel room in Arizona when I came to the undeniable conclusion that I was sick with a disorder that had originated in my head, not my body. The next doctor I visited was a psychiatrist, who had me complete a depression questionnaire.

The results concerned both of us.

Together, we concluded that my major life changes had made me deeply anxious, throwing my physiology out of equilibrium. Because of the inseparable connection between the mind and the body, the doctor explained, stress had provoked my immune system and had led to a dizzying array of symptoms.

The psychiatrist offered me a look of concern. "If you push your body and mind much further, I fear you'll get yourself into even bigger trouble."

Tears formed in my eyes unexpectedly. "What do you think I should do?"

He sat back in his chair and exhaled. "You're like a bear that left its cave and got its butt kicked. Maybe you should go back to your cave and lick your wounds?"

I put my head in my hands and cried softly. In that moment, I knew what I needed to do. I hated to give up on my adventure, but I had to accept that the path I'd chosen was unrealistic. I should've started my medical career when I graduated med school and explored creative writing on the side. Instead, I'd climbed a shaky ladder and tumbled off.

"I have to go back to Boston," I said between sobs.

The psychiatrist walked around his desk and placed his hand on my shoulder. "I think that's the right decision, Dr. Bloom."

Chapter Three

Driving back to Boston from Arizona, I visited every bookstore I could find. I bought dozens of books about people who had overcome complex illnesses—everything from radical remission from terminal cancers to curing treatment-resistant depression through ayahuasca and shamanistic ritual.

A memoir by Norman Cousins, an overworked newspaper editor, was especially intriguing. In his forties, Cousins had been stricken with ankylosing spondylitis, the autoimmune disorder I feared most. He'd come home from a work trip when he developed what ended up being chronic pain all over his body.

Despite being bedridden for months, Cousins rejected the doctors' predictions that he would be handicapped for the rest of his life and die at an early age. He found a physician who supported his commitment to curing himself through lifestyle changes, such as eating nutrient-dense food and supplementing with vitamins, including high doses of vitamin C. He put himself on a steady diet of funny movies, thinking that laughter was the best medicine and positive feelings would rebalance his chemistry and heal his body.

This book became a road map for me. I made similar lifestyle changes as Cousins, including supplementing with vitamin C and avoiding ultra-processed food, opting for highly nutritious options. I stopped watching the news and started watching funny movies instead.

It's possible that Cousin's "laughter therapy" shifted my physiology in a more positive direction, but it was also a form of distraction. I let go of monitoring every ache and pain, and it helped me stop obsessing over my symptoms. For instance, if my back started spasming, I'd just lie on my bed and watch a movie to rob the pain of attention.

Reading, especially fiction, also helped me escape from my painful reality. I must've read *The Hitchhiker's Guide to the Galaxy* some twenty times during my recovery. Reading something that took my mind away from my illness was potent medicine. Who knew that simple distraction could be so healing?

When I read nonfiction, I educated myself about psychosomatic illnesses or mind-body disorders. I learned how anxiety or depression could manifest as a wide array of symptoms: insomnia, fatigue, tremors, migraines, tingling limbs, numbness. I was especially interested in books that described the mechanics of how emotions caused physical symptoms, like a fascinating book by Dr. Candice Pert, who pioneered the biochemistry of emotions, and books by Dr. John Sarno, who explored how unexamined emotions like anger and sadness could trigger back pain and even autoimmune diseases.

When I returned to Boston, I reached out to my former landlord, who offered me my old studio, as it hadn't yet been rented. I eagerly accepted. Upon moving back into such familiar surroundings, I began to relax in a way I hadn't since leaving on my trip.

Once I'd settled back in, I found a therapist I liked and began to see him weekly. We discussed my decision to move across the country and the journey that followed. I came to realize that the experience was the first major failure of my life. As we talked, we created a coherent story that allowed me to regain a sense of control and loosen the grip the negative experiences had on my psyche.

Though I started to feel better mentally and emotionally, my body still hurt. I was convinced I'd never again be capable of activities like running or biking, but my primary care physician thought I could regain my former athleticism through physical therapy. The physical therapist I was referred to told me "motion was lotion" and led me through strengthening and stretching exercises twice a week. I also started swimming regularly.

As my muscles loosened and my body got stronger, I started to believe my chronic pain condition might go away. The unwavering faith of my therapist was, in part, therapeutic. He believed I'd once again be able to jog or sit at my desk and work without grinding back pain. This, in turn, helped me believe, and the self-fulfilling prophecy drove further recovery.

Two months in, my therapist asked if I'd started writing again.

"Not since I stopped to focus on my illness." I confessed that I might never write again.

"Why would you believe that about something you used to love?"

"I just feel like the drive to write has gone away."

Unsatisfied, my therapist coaxed me to talk about why I'd started writing in the first place and why I'd wanted to make a career of it. The conversation helped me remember how much joy I used to derive from the practice of writing.

Curious to see if I still could, I summoned the courage to sit at my computer one Saturday after a swim. I started typing, and before long, I'd completed the rough draft of a personal essay about my illness. I worked on the piece every day for a month, until I had a polished story of how I'd thought my way into illness and then thought my way back out. I sent the piece to a few publications and was delighted when it was accepted by a medical humanities journal that had previously published my fiction.

Months later, I was asked to give a lecture about my experience with psychosomatic illness at a psychiatric conference.

Six months into my recovery and almost back to normal, I turned my thoughts back to my future. I had to figure out what I was going to do with my medical degree. Yet there were too many possibilities and nothing that really called to me.

My indecision ended one night as I was watching a documentary. It followed a woman who struggled for years with chronic fatigue syndrome and other mysterious physical symptoms. I sympathized as she met with specialist after specialist to address the numbness in her limbs, the migraines, her irritable bowel syndrome, and her neck and back pain. She then met with a neurologist, who examined years of medical records in search of a pattern.

The neurologist, after reviewing her case, suggested that psychological or emotional issues might underlie her symptoms and that she might have a psychosomatic disorder, now called functional neurological disorder. When he broke the news, she interpreted his referral to a therapist as a dismissal of her *very real* physical symptoms. She left the hospital without answers, thinking she'd met another dead end. I saw my grandmother—and myself—in this case.

By the time the documentary ended, I was unsettled by the woman's inability to recognize that her illness might be influenced by her mind and emotions. I had made the connection, but, as I'd come to realize, some patients couldn't see so clearly.

In that moment, I knew the medical field I wanted to enter. I wanted to specialize in psychiatry and use the psychotherapeutic process to help others who got sick like I had but, for whatever reason, couldn't see the root causes of their illness.

Chapter Four

Months later, I was a psychiatry trainee at Boston's New England Psychological Services, one of the oldest and most respected mental health clinics in the country. Under the supervision of a more experienced psychiatrist, I worked with adults who had a variety of mental conditions, from generalized anxiety to bipolar disorder.

I'd thought choosing to specialize in psychiatry would solve my existential problems with medicine, but I was wrong. As a practicing psychiatrist, I discovered much of the treatment for mental health conditions relied on prescribing drugs. As such, I became little more than a manager of my patients' medications.

I realized I was more interested in psychotherapy because it involved talking with my patients to help them find ways to cope and manage their emotions through insights and self-discovery. But the existing system didn't afford me the time or resources to delve deeper into my patients' histories to understand what was really troubling them.

The problems with the field didn't stop there. Even if I'd known why my patients were sick, my medical training hadn't taught me how to help them activate their natural healing mechanisms. Medical school, I realized, wasn't about healing but rather, as one teacher had insisted, the diagnosis and treatment of diseases.

I expressed my frustration to colleagues during a staff meeting. "What if some mental disorders are perfectly legitimate responses to unhealthy habits or toxic conditions in our patients' lives?"

Nobody responded. They only stared at the papers in front of them, avoiding eye contact. Afterward, my colleagues began avoiding me. I started to feel like an outsider.

Clearly, nobody wanted to challenge the status quo of our chosen field. I began to think I'd made a terrible mistake returning to medicine, let alone choosing psychiatry.

Had I not met Dr. Arthur Pratt, I might have left medicine for good.

Needing a break from work, I decided to take a vacation. Fondly remembering my family's summer trips to Martha's Vineyard, I booked a room for a week at a bed-and-breakfast in West Tisbury, an artsy section of the island.

For the first couple of days, I explored the town, visiting local shops and strolling the beach. At night, I'd sit on the porch with a glass of wine and listen to the soothing sound of crashing waves as I reread old Michael Crichton novels.

On the third day, I ducked into the bed-and-breakfast's library before heading out for my morning walk. As I browsed the titles, one book caught my eye: *Paging Dr. Bratt: An Integrative Physician's Guide to Why We Get Sick and How We Can Stay Healthy.*

"Some books can change your life. That's one of them."

I turned to find Gloria, the owner of the bed-and-breakfast, sweeping the library's floor.

"How so?" I asked.

"My husband suffered from lupus for years," Gloria said, continuing to sweep. "We went to specialists at all the fancy Boston hospitals. He tried every treatment, nothing worked. Dr. Pratt saw him, and within a few months, my husband was cured."

Cured was a strong word. Lupus had no known cure and was difficult to manage. Nonetheless, I was curious. "What worked for your husband?"

A bell rang out from the front of the building. "I've got to help someone out," Gloria said, excusing herself. "Just read the book. Dr. Pratt's a genius!"

Turning the book over, I scanned the jacket curiously. According to his bio, Arthur "Art" Pratt, MD, was a retired doctor who'd practiced integrative medicine. His views weren't widely accepted by mainstream medicine, and those colleagues who considered him a radical called him Dr. "Bratt." Hence "The Bratt," a title he'd come to embrace as a badge of honor for questioning a broken healthcare system.

Feeling a bit like a radical myself, I decided to read the book. I dropped it in my bag and walked to the nearest coffee shop.

With an iced coffee in hand, I grabbed a seat by the window overlooking the ocean and started reading Dr. Pratt's book. It was so engrossing that I finished the first chapter without looking up once.

I admired the doctor's sincerity. He believed hospitals were only good for fixing problems that had already developed and were ill-equipped to prevent disease. "Chronically ill patients," he wrote, "should never step foot in a Western hospital."

His perspective was refreshing and reaffirmed my own recent thoughts. I, too, felt I wasn't helping my patients in the best ways possible. I, too, wanted to prevent patients from developing conditions, not just treat them. I, too, had begun to feel like an outsider.

Dr. Pratt had spent decades as a rheumatologist, but most of his patients never got any better, living miserably with their conditions for years. Fed up, he left his job at a major hospital in Boston, moved to the Vineyard, and opened his own clinical practice specializing in integrative medicine.

One of his first patients, Naomi, suffered from unexplained stomach pains that world-renowned gastroenterologists in New York City couldn't diagnose, let alone begin to treat effectively. Some doctors suspected a cyst or Crohn's disease, but tests always came back inconclusive. The doctors eventually settled on irritable bowel syndrome, a diagnosis given to patients with gastrointestinal symptoms of unknown origin.

"When I first met Naomi," Dr. Pratt wrote, "I threw everything I'd learned about medicine out the window. My main concern was trying to understand her and the conditions in her life that could be contributing to her problems. I blocked off an hour in my schedule just to focus on her and her story."

Before the visit, Dr. Pratt reviewed Naomi's medical chart, which reported numerous visits to specialists and many medical interventions. "I resisted the powerful urge to accept the conclusions of other doctors. I intended to create my own."

When they first met, Dr. Pratt turned his chair away from his computer, made direct eye contact with Naomi, and invited her to tell him her story. "I'm going to be your doctor, so I'd like you to tell me what you think I should know about your situation."

He let Naomi talk, not even interrupting her to ask questions. "I learned more in the first ten minutes than I could have after an hour studying her chart."

Naomi, he learned, was a senior vice president at a publishing company in Manhattan. She worked twelve-hour days under high-pressure conditions, and usually went to bed around midnight, often sleeping restlessly. She didn't exercise as much as she wanted and hadn't seen a vegetable in years.

"By the time Naomi finished telling her story, I strongly believed her stressful lifestyle was driving her physical symptoms," Dr. Pratt wrote. "How could any human being *not* develop symptoms under such conditions? Now, if I'd been practicing in the city, I might have treated her GI symptoms with a prescription medication. Instead, I did something I'd never done. No joke, I wrote *walk in the woods* on a prescription pad, tore off the page, and handed it to her. I directed her to a common hiking spot on the Vineyard."

"You want to me just . . . go to the woods and . . . walk?" Naomi asked.

"That's right," Dr. Pratt replied. "Walk slowly and quietly and note what's going on around you. Stop somewhere, close your eyes, and focus on senses other than sight for a few minutes."

Naomi was skeptical, but she followed her doctor's orders. A few hours later, she returned to Dr. Pratt's office looking less frazzled, and her face was bright with energy. Better yet, her stomach didn't ache anymore.

"Are those trees giving off antidepressants or what?" she asked.

Dr. Pratt explained that Naomi had just taken part in "forest bathing," a practice that involved spending time in quiet contemplation in natural places. It had originated in Japan in 1982 as a national program called shinrin-yoku, which meant spending time around trees. Since then, the healing practice had been scientifically proven to reduce stress and anxiety, increase mental clarity, and improve sleep.

"How can a forest affect my body and mind?" Naomi asked.

Dr. Pratt explained how trees and plants emitted chemicals to protect themselves from microorganisms and insects. Some of these chemicals, known as phytocides, affected the human body by lowering blood pressure, heart rate, and stress hormones and boosting the body's ability to fight infection and even cancer.

"The forest is like a pharmacy," Naomi replied.

"Exactly!"

Dr. Pratt was pleased that Naomi's stomach symptoms had gone away after spending time in nature. However, he predicted the relief would only be temporary since she'd soon return to the same stressful work conditions that had made her sick in the first place.

"If you don't have anything on your calendar for the rest of the day," Dr. Pratt told Naomi, "why don't you spend the rest of the afternoon just relaxing on the beach?"

Naomi was reluctant. "I was hoping to get some work done."

The doctor explained that the best treatment for exhaustion was simple: doing nothing. "Why is it so hard for us to slow down and pause for a little while?" he wrote. "The American motto 'as much as possible, as fast as possible' is making us sick!"

Realizing her work could wait, Naomi went to the beach.

Dr. Pratt joined her after seeing his last patient, and they relaxed and talked for hours. Naomi "trauma bombed" Dr. Pratt, dumping her painful experiences onto him all at once, but instead of scorning her for it, he welcomed her stories. He believed that letting a patient—or anyone, really—unburden themselves could be therapeutic.

Naomi described her romantic life as an utter mess. She'd dated, but had found men in New York City to be immature and noncommittal. A few had been narcissists, proficient in making everything about themselves. Some had been psychologically abusive. All of it had shaken her self-esteem and self-confidence.

"I let Naomi say what she wanted—*needed*—to say, only briefly interrupting a few times to ask clarifying questions. After a few hours, she looked like she'd taken off a fifty-pound backpack."

She ended up extending her stay on the island, spending a week in a vacation rental close to Dr. Pratt's cottage. Together, they created a healing plan that involved daily walks, morning meditations, and radical changes to her diet.

The integrative physician talked a lot about nutrition in his book. He cited the well-documented toxicity of the standard American diet, which was too low in lean protein, healthy oils, and fresh fruits and vegetables, and too high in processed foods, high-fat dairy products, red meat, refined carbohydrates, added sugars and salt. He considered it scandalous that nutrition wasn't a bigger part of medical training and tragic that too few healthcare providers used food to help their patients get better.

At the end of the third chapter, Dr. Pratt evoked the father of medicine, Hippocrates: *Let food be thy medicine and medicine be thy food.*

Once I'd finished the chapter, I stared dreamily out the window for several minutes, staggered by Dr. Pratt's ideas. This book was a revelation! His approach to medicine was simple but profound. He'd said everything I'd been wanting to say but hadn't yet found the language for. He just listened to Naomi's story and suggested simple lifestyle changes that calmed her body and mind, resolving her symptoms.

So often, I'd wanted to suggest similar changes to my patients' lives. For a patient with frequent migraines, for instance, I'd wanted to drive home the importance of maintaining a healthy routine to keep their systems in relative balance. For anxiety, I'd wished I could get across that it might be a strong signal that something was wrong in the patient's life and that addressing what was troubling them could lead to positive change.

I continued reading and learned that many of Dr. Pratt's patients had gotten better when they simply stopped doing what had made them sick. "If you're in a ditch," he wrote, "stop digging." He believed most patients could heal their diseases with their bodies' natural warehouse of chemicals. The role of the healthcare provider was simply to help patients activate their inner pharmacy, which would heal their bodies from within.

Such theories would've been brushed off by my colleagues, but I was intrigued by Dr. Pratt's theories and methods.

A few hours later, I returned to the bed-and-breakfast. As I walked through the front door, Gloria bounced gleefully behind the desk. "So?"

"Hard to put down, honestly," I said.

"So glad to hear it! It must be interesting reading it as a doctor?"

"Absolutely. I've been trying to find my own voice as a psychiatrist, and I find his holistic approach to healing inspiring. I also found Naomi's story compelling."

"Oh, we love Naomi around here."

"What do you mean?"

Gloria raised an eyebrow. "How far are you in the book?"

"About halfway."

"Oh, honey, you haven't gotten to the best part yet. Naomi never left!"

"Never left . . . the Vineyard?"

Gloria nodded excitedly. "Dr. Pratt and Naomi have been married for thirty years!" She leaned in close, lowering her voice. "Some people think it's quite the scandal, given that she was his patient, but I think it's a beautiful love story."

It was unusual, but there weren't any laws against it.

"Where do they live?" I asked.

"At the edge of town in a small beach cottage. The one with the yellow siding."

"For some reason, I just assumed Dr. Pratt had passed away."

"Oh, please." Gloria giggled. "The man's eighty-six going on thirty-six."

Laughing, I thanked her for the book recommendation. I went up to my room to continue reading and finished the book around midnight.

The next morning, I was returning the book to the bed-and-breakfast's library when Gloria yelled from the front desk, "He loves drop-ins, you know!"

I poked my head around the corner. "Who does?"

"Dr. Pratt! People come from all over the world to visit him," she said. "His 'disciples,' Naomi calls them. You should swing by their cottage."

"I doubt he needs another stranger on his doorstep."

"Nonsense! He loves meeting new people. Plus, you're a doctor. He loves talking about medicine and how the healthcare system could be better."

To meet the man who'd written such an inspiring book was tempting, but it was my last day on the island and I wanted to rent a bike to explore.

When I told Gloria as much, she shrugged. "Suit yourself."

Chapter Five

Later that morning, I rode a bike along a coastal path, enjoying the warm spring sunshine on my face. I was trying to enjoy the view, but I couldn't stop thinking about Dr. Pratt's ideas about medicine and healing; I was fooling myself if I thought I didn't want to know more. I turned around and steered my bike to the edge of town.

When I reached the cottage with yellow siding, I leaned my bike against a fence. Climbing the steps up to the porch, I knocked on the front door, but no one answered. I heard faint laughter, so I followed it around the house to the back and found an elderly couple playing bocce ball on a bright-green lawn.

I cleared my throat to get their attention. "Um, hello there."

An elderly man with a bald head and fluffy white beard frowned dramatically and pointed at me. "Naomi, we have an intruder! Call the cops!"

Freezing in place, I put my hands up. "Oh, I'm really sorry. I just—"

The man threw his head back and laughed, placing a hand on his potbelly. "I'm kidding, fella!" He waved me onto the lawn and looked me up and down. "Who do we have here?"

"Another disciple, I presume," the woman said.

"My name's Dr. Calvin Bloom. I'm a psychiatrist at New England Psychological Services in Boston. I just finished reading your book, and the owner of the bed-and-breakfast I'm staying at said you didn't mind people dropping by."

"Gloria's always sending us fine folks like yourself. I'm Arthur and this is"—he gestured to the woman—"my lovely wife, Naomi."

I shook their hands. "It's wonderful to meet you both."

As I stepped back, I eyed Arthur's loose-fitting Hawaiian shirt.

Chuckling, he tugged at the ocean-blue fabric. "When you're retired, you can wear whatever you want."

Naomi looked skyward, pretending to be offended. "No matter how many polos I lay out for him, he always goes for the Hawaiians."

Arthur grumbled. "You try wearing a stuffy white coat for forty years!"

"Oh, please. Try wearing high heels! You wouldn't last an hour."

Glancing at me, Arthur nodded. "When she's right, she's right." He scanned the lawn. "You play bocce ball, Calvin?"

"I've played before, yes."

Arthur walked to a rectangular box on the lawn, opened the cover, and pulled out two orange balls. He handed them to me. "Fire away."

I glanced at Naomi, who nodded toward the target—a small black ball called the *pallino*—about fifteen feet away. "Give it your best shot, doc."

We played for an hour, talking about a variety of things, from politics to movies. After a few games, they invited me to stay for dinner. It was Mexican night at the Pratt household, and they were making burritos.

Sitting at a small table on the cottage's back deck overlooking a beach, we ate and drank freshly made margaritas. I told Arthur how much I'd enjoyed his book and that I, too, had an interest in writing about medicine and patients, though in fiction. I told him I'd had a few short stories published but had stopped writing fiction after my cross-country trip.

"I love medical fiction," Arthur said, rolling the contents of his burrito into a tight wrap. "Who knows. Maybe something will get the pen moving again."

Naomi licked salt from the rim of her glass. "Tell us more about this trip."

"When I got out of med school, I didn't know what to do next. It sounds corny, but taking an adventure was a way for me to lose myself so I could find myself. And I did figure out where I wanted to take my medical career; I just paid a fairly high price for it."

"How so, if you don't mind me asking?" Naomi asked.

"All the stress of an uncertain path led to some physical symptoms that I initially thought might be an autoimmune disorder. It took a while, but I eventually realized that I was experiencing a problem of the mind, not the body."

Arthur nodded knowingly. "The human body is infinitely creative in its ability to produce symptoms, but if you listen to them, try to understand where they're coming from, they might tell you something important, something you needed to know."

"At first, I lost perspective and fixated on my symptoms, convinced I was going crazy. Eventually, I saw them for what they were—and I got better."

"Sounds like something worth writing about," Naomi said.

"Couldn't agree more," Arthur added.

"I actually published my story in a medical journal."

Arthur raised his glass. "Here, here!"

We all drank from our glasses.

For a few moments, we just sat silently and admired the sound of waves crashing on the beach. I thought about how lucky I'd been to stumble on Arthur's book and how gracious he and Naomi had been to invite me into their home.

Arthur broke the silence to start a discussion about other doctors who were also writers. "Who are some of your favorites, Cal?"

I talked about my long fascination with physicians who wrote fiction, like Anton Chekhov, Arthur Conan Doyle, and Michael Crichton.

Arthur recommended I read the work of doctors who wrote nonfiction, especially his favorite, Atul Gawande, a surgeon and public health researcher who wrote books and articles about his profession for lay readers.

"I've been meaning to read Oliver Sacks's books," I told them. "He recently passed away, but he wrote about the fascinating illnesses of his patients."

"Sacks is a legend," Arthur said, sipped at his margarita. "Though some are saying he might've made up some of the details about his patients."

"I hadn't heard that. That's why I like fiction. You can just make stuff up."

"Ever read *When Breath Becomes Air?*" Naomi asked.

I shook my head and used my fork to collect rice that had fallen out of my burrito.

"It's an incredibly touching memoir by a neurosurgeon who wrote about his struggle with terminal cancer at the peak of his surgical career," Arthur said.

"I cried the whole way through," Naomi added.

"I like how the author wove together stories of his patients and philosophical reflections," Arthur said. "We spend so much time ignoring the fact that we're all going to die; the story helps us face that denial and reminds us we should make the most of our lives."

Finishing my burrito, I wiped my mouth with a napkin. "If you don't mind me asking, Arthur—"

He raised a hand, interrupting me. "Call me Art, please."

I nodded. "Very well . . . Art. How'd you get started writing?"

"I'd always wanted to be a writer. But when I took a writing class at Harvard, the teacher compared us all to Hemingway and Fitzgerald. I got a D, the first one I'd ever gotten in school. So, I stopped writing in college. When I graduated, I got a Rhodes Scholarship to Oxford, and that's when

I started to write seriously."

"What brought you to medicine?"

Arthur tipped back the glass and finished his margarita. "When I got back from the UK, I applied to med school. I wanted to keep writing, but I needed a way to pay the bills and I thought medicine could do that. I didn't want to write for money. If I did, I might've had to write for TV or movies, and that didn't interest me. For years, I worked in hospitals and wrote articles and short case histories."

He gestured toward me. "You know, psychiatry is a great specialty for burgeoning writers, Calvin. You're constantly learning about people and hearing great stories."

"And you don't have to start your day until the afternoon, if you want," Naomi said with a chuckle.

I laughed, then asked Arthur how he decided what to write about.

He raised a finger in the air. "I became disenchanted with medicine early in my career. I became a doctor in the sixties, and my idealism smacked up against the healthcare hierarchy, which was primarily concerned with making money. The process of becoming a doctor is horrible. It's a cruel, brutal system, so I decided to write about the injustices I saw in the training we undergo to become doctors."

"I know exactly what you're talking about," I said. "Everyone I trained with in med school got so isolated from people outside the hospital because of the time schedules. We eventually got isolated from each other, then ourselves."

"Absolutely. I wanted to get the message out to the world. So, I just put my experiences down on paper."

"It's such grim subject matter—loneliness, alienation, life and death— but your book is quite funny. How did you decide to inject humor into it?"

"I realized that what got us all through our training was humor—gallows humor. Our circumstances were so brutal, we used humor to manage our suffering."

"Not to mention," Naomi added, "no one would've read it if it wasn't funny."

Arthur chuckled. "That's for sure."

With all my questions, I was starting to feel like a reporter, but I was genuinely interested, and Arthur didn't seem to mind my inquiries.

"What was your process for writing the book?"

"I got all the doctors I trained with in a room," he said. "We drank beers and smoked pot, and I tape-recorded our conversations as we reminisced about our training."

"Did your book lead to any changes in the process of training doctors?"

"It did, but I paid a high price for it. I was on the faculty at Harvard Med when the book came out, and they came after me—did some nasty stuff. Luckily, NYU called me and asked me to join their faculty and teach lessons from my book."

"What's your take on medicine today?"

"It's gotten better, but the healthcare system's still deeply broken. I feel like medicine can go one of two ways: toward more humane care or toward the almighty dollar and more computer screens, which are basically designed to make as much money as possible by billing the insurance companies."

Naomi kneed Arthur playfully under the table. "Tell him about your *new* book."

"Right, right." He leaned forward in his seat. "I want to inspire the system to put humanity back in medicine."

"How so?" I asked.

"I'm trying to reimagine the typical doctor's visit. See, we thought screens would allow us to deal with data better, and they did, but the problem is that the insurance companies got their fingers in the pie to monetize the data. Now, healthcare providers are chained to these machines, and that's *not* why we became doctors."

Arthur's perspective resonated. "When I was rounding in medical school, there was always a competition with the computer. We called it the 'third actor in the room.'"

He smiled. "The doctor enters the exam room, barely makes eye contact with their patient, and sits hunched in front of a screen the whole visit. They ask questions; the patient answers. I want to talk and listen to my patient and be their doctor, not sit in front of a machine all day. Patients don't want us doing that either!"

"It's like the healthcare system forgot about us."

Arthur nodded. "We no longer have a *we* in healthcare. It should never be what *I* or *you* are going to do. I've always used the word *we*. I'll say to a patient, 'What are we going to do about this problem?' And the patient will say, 'I think *we* should do this.' That's how to connect with patients. It should be mutual."

"I like the idea of developing the quality of our connections with patients."

"If you don't connect with your patients, you won't get their full stories." Arthur gestured toward me. "Do you know what most patients who sue their doctors say?"

I shook my head.

"They say they didn't have a good relationship with their doctor." He pressed his elbow into Naomi's side. "Isn't that right, dear?"

She rolled her eyes.

"Trying to connect with your patients can be messy," I said. "It's hard to know if you're ever getting it right."

"You're never going to get every patient interaction perfect, Cal. But if you take a *we* perspective, you can go through anything with your patients."

I admired Arthur's passion and vision. I found the whole conversation, the whole evening, inspirational. "I'd really love to write something that has the kind of impact you've had, but I guess I haven't found something worth writing about."

"But you said you've published some of your work, right?" Naomi asked.

"I have, but I can't imagine more than a few hundred people read them."

Naomi covered Arthur's hand with her own. "Any advice for the young man?"

The veteran doctor sat back thoughtfully. "The only reason to write seriously is if you can't *not* write about something. The medical system forced me to write. I couldn't *not* write that book. I see something and say, 'This isn't right. Somebody needs to write about it.' If you pick a project that puts fire in your belly, the work will carry you through. You won't have to carry *it*."

I nodded and thanked him for the advice.

Arthur eyed me for a moment. "If you don't mind me asking, could I read the story you wrote about your illness?"

"Of course," I replied and told him where he could find it online.

"I look forward to reading it." Arthur hummed. "You might also want to look into narrative medicine."

That sounded vaguely familiar; I urged Arthur to explain further.

He said narrative medicine encouraged clinicians to write and share stories of clinical encounters with one another. The field's founder, Dr. Rita Charon, believed that by studying literature and other arts, healthcare providers could develop deeper psychological insights and sensitivities, allowing them to better listen to their patients.

By the end of his explanation, Naomi let out a soft yawn. Realizing it was late, I said I should get going and helped Arthur and Naomi bring the dishes into the kitchen.

We walked to the front door, and Arthur shook my hand. "It's been a pleasure, Dr. Bloom. Best of luck with everything, and feel free to reach out anytime."

Naomi hugged me. "You're always welcome back."

"I'll definitely stay in touch."

Chapter Six

Ireturned from Martha's Vineyard with a renewed focus for my work. In the words of Oliver Wendell Holmes Sr., my mind had been stretched by Arthur's vision of medicine, and it refused to shrink "back to its former dimensions."

Emboldened, I began exploring different methods for treating patients with psychiatric conditions. It would've been reckless to experiment with their medications, but I was no longer quick to write a prescription for anti-depressants or antianxiety drugs. Instead, I practiced Dr. Pratt's approach, asking new patients to tell me their stories, and suggesting lifestyle changes that might help.

To my delight, Arthur and I started speaking regularly over video calls. The retired physician became a trusted friend and mentor. He was especially helpful when I was having difficulties with a patient.

"One of the hardest things for clinicians to accept is that sometimes, we can try every drug, every intervention and nothing seems to work," Arthur said on a call. "We can feel ineffective when we have nothing else to offer a patient."

"I hate feeling that way," I told him. "I'm a doctor; it's my job to help identify people's problems and treat them."

He recommended a book about an English general practitioner in the late sixties named John Sassall who cared for patients with great compassion. "It's a meditation on the role a doctor plays in society."

"And what role is that?"

"We can't always provide a remedy for what's ailing our patients,

Calvin, but we can always treat our patients with respect and humanity."

Arthur's perspective brought me comfort. But I still couldn't shake the feeling that I could be doing more for my patients, especially those with severe psychiatric illnesses. What happens when you run out of solutions for the sickest in your care? What if psychiatry needed a new healing approach?

About a year after meeting Arthur, I took a day trip on a Sunday to Concord to visit Walden Pond to do a little forest bathing of my own. Arriving in the late afternoon, I parked and wandered down to the water, where a path circled the pond. It was a gorgeous spring day; the flowers were in bloom, and the temperature had climbed to the midsixties.

After about half an hour of following the water's edge, I came across a narrow offshoot of the path that led deeper into Walden Woods. Feeling adventurous, I plunged into the forest.

I'd been walking for a while when the path broke out of the tree line. The setting sun revealed a small field at the far end of which sat an old, dilapidated building. Its windows were boarded up and its roof had collapsed in a few spots.

Curious, I pulled out my phone and, finding I had service, opened a map of the area to see if I could figure out what the building had once been. Turns out, it was the Concord Almshouse, a 1960s psychiatric institution that had closed when a state-sponsored investigation found that inmates were being treated cruelly.

My mind churned as I stared, dazed, at the neglected facility. Possibilities swirled in my mind, too many and too fanciful to be anything more than daydreams.

As I headed back toward my car later, my phone buzzed in my pocket. No doubt, it was my grandmother's usual Sunday call, a bit later than usual, but I was excited to tell her about the mysterious building I'd happened upon in the woods.

When I pulled out my phone, I didn't recognize the number. When I answered, an unfamiliar voice spoke. "Calvin Bloom?"

"This is him," I said.

"My name's Patrick Anderson, and I'm a lawyer with Hale and Anderson. I'm the fiduciary handling Edith Bloom's affairs."

"Uh… I'm not sure I understand."

"I'm sorry to inform you, but your grandmother passed away last night."

My stomach dropped. I'd known this day was coming, but I hadn't been prepared for it. I didn't catch much else the lawyer said, except that he'd follow up with an email explaining next steps.

When I hung up, I looked back at the darkened forest. I thought about my grandmother, who never got the help she needed for her health issues, never fully understanding their causes, and how she suffered because of it.

In that moment, I was struck by a fierce need to find a way to help patients who didn't respond to modern medical techniques. The next thought that popped into my mind was preposterous, probably impossible, and yet its grip was too tight on my psyche to ignore it. I realized what I needed to do. What I was *meant* to do.

I had to find a way to transform that abandoned building into a cutting-edge mental health center, where I could practice medicine the way I wanted. Maybe then I could help those people who slipped through the cracks of the healthcare system.

Chapter Seven

Weeks later, I waited in the clearing for the realtor who'd agreed to show me around the old building. When he emerged from the makeshift trail I'd created to reach the area, he looked down and frowned at his boat shoes, which were covered in mud. He stomped his feet in frustration, muttering, "Damn it."

Clearly, Mr. Boat Shoes didn't spend a lot of time in the woods. In a navy-blue polo and corduroy pants, he might as well have just gotten off the ferry from Nantucket.

Once he was done, he spotted me and waved, ambling closer. "Dr. Bloom, I presume? Nice to meet you. I'm Brandon; we spoke on the phone."

I shook his hand. "I hope it wasn't too much trouble getting here?"

He swatted away a black fly, looking uncomfortable. "No, I always enjoy spending time in the great outdoors."

I gestured toward the old building. "Shall we?"

"Let's do it." He led me toward the front door. "I was surprised to get your call."

"Yeah?"

"Most people who ask about this place just want to knock it down. But the seller is adamant that the buyer keep it standing." Once on the porch, Brandon fished for the key in his pocket. "I'm curious, though. How'd you even find it?"

"I was just strolling through the woods and stumbled on it."

"Hmm, all right. You said you're a psychiatrist?"

I nodded.

"And you want to create some kind of wellness center?"

"Not quite," I said. "A modern psychotherapeutic practice."

"Gotcha." Brandon used the key to unlock the door. "You're lucky. Most of this area is state reservation, which prohibits the creation of private businesses, but this property is in Adams Woods, not Walden Woods."

As the door swung open, a strong musty scent with a hint of antiseptic swept over us. The realtor waved a hand in front of his face. "We might need to air the place out."

The building screamed abandoned asylum. It had an atmosphere of stark, clinical efficiency, and the hallways Brandon led me down were lined with sterile, white walls. He opened doors to show me sparsely furnished rooms, some of which still had institutional metal-framed beds and wooden chairs.

I pointed to a sturdy wooden door, weathered with age, that looked like it might lead to a basement. "What's down there?"

He looked left and right and then leaned closer, as if he were about to tell me a secret. "Rumor has it, that's where they kept 'problem patients' and did all sorts of now-banned treatments, like lobotomies and other experimental stuff."

I shook my head in disbelief. I hadn't read that the institution had done lobotomies. I'd never been able to comprehend how such an invasive practice was once accepted, even considered cutting-edge treatment at one point. "It's heartbreaking—infuriating, really—to think about patients having to endure such barbaric treatments."

Brandon nodded, suddenly looking uneasy, and knocked on the door casually. "Good for storage, though."

I glanced at the stairwell next to the door. "There's living space upstairs, right?"

"Let the tour continue." Brandon led me up the stairs, which opened onto a small living room, and down a hallway across from the stairs. Opening a door at the end of the hall, he revealed an empty studio apartment. "Small, but cozy."

The room was small and simple, but I could see myself living there.

In the middle of the room, Brandon put his hands on his hips. "Well, that's pretty much it, Dr. Bloom." His eyes widened in realization. "Oh wait, I forgot the best part!"

Leading me back down the hallway, he opened a door to the right of the stairs, revealing a back deck that faced the woods. We walked onto the second-floor deck. The sun was setting, and the forest was dark and humming with night creatures.

Brandon stuck his nose in the air. "You can practically smell the smoke from Henry David Thoreau's fire, right?"

I laughed, but I imagined the rugged writer, sitting by a small fire beside his tiny cabin, not far from where we were. Staring into the dark forest from the deck, I actually thought of something Thoreau had once written:

> *You must live in the present, launch yourself on every wave, find your eternity in each moment. Fools stand on their island of opportunities and look toward another land. There is no other land; there is no other life but this.*

I leaned over the railing, mulling over Thoreau's words, and felt something stir deep within my soul. In that moment, I had a strong sense that I was on the right path, as if transforming this forgotten building into a mental-health center was my destiny.

Brandon snapped his fingers in front of my face, startling me back to the here and now. "So, what do you think, Dr. Bloom?"

"I want it," I said without thinking.

The realtor looked me up and down. "Price is two million."

I tried to keep my reaction in check so he wouldn't think I'd wasted his time, but the price nearly knocked the wind out of me. My grandmother had left me some money, but even with a mortgage, I wouldn't be able to afford the place. I stared at Brandon's muddy shoes, not knowing what to say, until I blurted out, "I can work with that."

When I looked back at Brandon, his eyebrows were raised.

"Give me a few days to move some money," I added.

Brandon's face curled into a grin, as if his commission had already hit his checking account. "I'll start drawing up the papers."

* * *

That night, I called Arthur to seek his advice. When he answered, he was walking on the beach near his cottage on the Vineyard, sipping from a margarita by the sound of it. I told him I'd found a great property near Walden Pond and had a vision for turning it into a cutting-edge psychiatric institution.

"What kind of shape is the building in?" he asked.

"It's pretty beat up—needs a new roof, plumbing and electricity work, some other basic stuff—but I think it could be something great."

"You should go for it, Cal."

I was pleased to have Arthur's endorsement, but it was way out of reach.

He seemed to sense that something was wrong. "What's the catch?"

I laughed self-consciously. "To be honest, it's the cost. I'm a bit short."

He hummed. "What's the price tag?"

"Two million."

Arthur didn't respond right away. When he did, his tone was gentle. "Is this what you really want?"

"Absolutely," I said confidently. "I want to help the most difficult-to-treat mental health patients, and I need to start my own practice to do it right."

After another silence, Arthur seemed to come to a decision. "I want to help you, Calvin, because I can tell you genuinely want to help people. I'm getting old and I can't take my money with me when I shove off, so if this is really what you want, I'd be happy to loan you the money you need."

I hadn't expected him to say that. "Oh, Art, you don't—"

"Happy to do it," he said. "I know you'll do great things."

I was so grateful. But I also felt pressured to make Arthur proud. I exhaled, not knowing exactly what to say.

"What's the matter?" he asked. "This is a happy moment!"

I tried to put words to my apprehension. "I've only ever been a clinician; I've never run a clinic before. What if it's too overwhelming? What if it's all too much for me? I could . . . break down again."

Arthur adopted a reassuring tone. "Look, I was nervous, too, when I first opened my clinic, but I just worked my butt off and took it day by day, and it worked out."

Thanking him, I hung up and set the phone down. For a few minutes, I just stared off into the distance. My dream was actually going to happen.

A few days later, I met with a banker to figure out the financing. Arthur's loan helped me cover the down payment and renovations on the building, and I took out a sizable mortgage to cover the rest of the costs. A day later, I signed the paperwork, and though I was exhausted, I felt satisfied.

The daydream I'd had in the woods was finally on its way to becoming real. It hadn't been in time to help my grandmother, but I could help others like her see their illnesses for what they were: not always physical diseases but products of their minds.

With Brandon's help, I found an architect who helped me redesign the building, which originally accommodated 350 beds, into a more modest 2,600-square-foot facility. The reduced footprint would create more natural space for patients to connect with nature.

When renovations finished a few months later, the building had a welcoming consultation room for me and my patients, two offices for a nurse and another staff member, a kitchen, and an unfinished basement.

As the move-in date approached, I felt a mix of excitement and nervousness for the adventure ahead.

Chapter Eight

About a month before I was set to leave New England Psycholog-ical Services and move into the apartment in my new facility, I got a referral for a female patient in her midthirties. When I told her I was moving my practice to Concord, she said the twenty-minute drive from her apartment in Cambridge would be fine for once-a-week sessions.

The first thing I noticed about Kendall was her piercing green eyes. Then there was her hair—straight, black, and falling to her upper back like ink spilling across a blank page.

In our first session, she seemed tense, afraid to speak her mind. When I asked what she did for work, she told me she wrote and managed corporate communications at a hospital in Newton.

"Do you like it?"

"It's fine. It's a job. I take pride in the work, but I've always wanted to write something more creative. Something with my own name on it."

I recorded her comments in my notebook. "Why do you think it's been difficult to write something of your own?"

"I've written in the hospital's voice for so long, I guess I lost mine."

"Have you tried to write creatively?"

She nodded. "But it's never any good, so I never get far."

"Why do you think that?"

She shrugged. "Because it's true? I don't feel like I have a talent for creative writing, and it's not like anyone is interested in any of the story ideas I've tried."

During the session, we explored why Kendall might be creatively blocked. She shared a few relevant memories of colleagues and family members telling her she was a mediocre writer, especially her father. She'd also been convinced she couldn't earn a living from writing (something I had to learn the hard way). Thoughts like these always came up whenever she put pen to paper.

At the end of the appointment, I asked her what she thought of therapy so far.

She just shrugged.

In our next appointment, we talked more about Kendall's work life. When she admitted she didn't have a good buffer between her work and personal life, I thought about how Arthur prescribed forest bathing to Naomi to calm her nervous system.

"Would you be open to trying something?"

"Like what?"

"It's been shown that engaging in a period of rest in the outdoors can relax people experiencing stress. Is there a state park or a trail system where you live?"

Kendall eyed me skeptically. "My roommate likes to take her dog to Middlesex Fells. A lot of people go there to get away from the city."

I'd been to the Fells several times, fifteen minutes north of Boston, where forest, wetlands, and rugged hills stretched for over two thousand acres. I asked her to go there over the weekend, spend a few hours walking around.

"Whatever you say, Doc."

* * *

A week later, Kendall walked into our next appointment and spoke up before she was even fully seated. "Well, I walked around the forest for a couple of hours on Sunday morning, just like you asked."

I leaned forward eagerly. "And how'd it go?"

"I got more bug bites than inspiration."

Recognizing her sarcasm, I sat back in my seat, and decided to take a different tack. "Do you have a sense of what drives your desire to write?"

To my surprise, she brought up her father. "We never exactly got along. He was too much of a loser."

"In what way?"

"Never did anything with his life. Bounced from job to job, spent years unemployed, just sat around watching movies or riding his tractor in the backyard."

I started to wonder whether her reason for doing therapy had less to do with her desire to write and more to do with her relationship with her father.

"What did you want him to do?" I asked.

"I don't know, examine himself? Find out what he wanted to do with his life."

"You think if he'd looked inward, he might've found his place in the world?"

"Maybe. I just know I'll end up lost like him if I don't figure out my own stuff. That's why I'm here. I'm doing what he never had the guts to."

"You talk about your dad in the past tense. He passed away?"

She averted her eyes. "Heart attack."

"Do you want to talk about it?"

She shook her head and remained silent.

A few weeks into therapy, I asked Kendall something I ask most patients early in treatment: "What do you think will help you?"

"I hate to break it to you, Dr. Bloom, but it ain't forest baths. I didn't have the heart to tell you at the time, but I don't even like the outdoors."

"That so?"

"A few years ago, I was on a camping trip in Maine with friends. I was bitten by a tick and ended up with Lyme disease. I never got the rash, so by the time the doctors figured out what it was, the bacteria had already gone dormant, and I'd developed chronic Lyme."

Curious whether her Lyme infection could be contributing to her mental health, I asked, "What kinds of symptoms did you experience?"

"Intense flu-like symptoms for a few days, but most of them went away after a few months. To this day if I overexert myself, the bacteria rears its ugly head and I become extremely tired. Sometimes, I can't get out of bed for days."

"Do you think the infection has any other effects on your body?"

She nodded solemnly. "Yeah, but you're not going to believe me."

"Try me."

"A few months after the tick bite, I had a barbecue at my house. I cooked all kinds of meat: hotdogs, burgers, sausages, even a porterhouse steak. That night, I had terrible stomach cramps. I felt like I was going to faint, and had this feeling of impending doom."

"Did you see a doctor?"

Kendall shook her head. "I eventually got to sleep. The next morning, I felt groggy, but I was mostly back to normal, so I just moved on. A week later, I cooked pork chops for dinner as an experiment, and it happened again. I felt woozy and light-headed, couldn't catch my breath. I went to the bathroom and saw I had a rash on my neck. When I lifted my shirt, my stomach was covered in hives."

"Sounds like an allergic reaction."

"That's what I thought. Since it seemed to be related to eating meat, I googled 'meat allergy.' I didn't think it was a thing, but I found an arti-cle about a guy who'd actually developed one. My primary care doctor dismissed the idea, though, saying people don't develop allergies to foods they've eaten their whole lives."

Classic, I thought. A doctor dismisses a patient's symptoms because they haven't heard of them before. "Was the man you read about bitten by a tick?"

She gave a nod. "It turns out a lot of people have been reporting sudden allergies to meat after being bitten by ticks."

"Do they know what causes the reaction?"

"Apparently, when a tick bites you, among other things, it injects a sugar molecule called alpha-gal into your bloodstream. The immune system attacks it, making you feel awful. It can cause a chronic condition called alpha-gal syndrome, or AGS. So, I have Lyme *and* AGS."

"I'm guessing there's alpha-gal in meat?"

"Yup. A year went by, and I decided to try meat again, thinking the allergy might have gone away. Terrible idea. I spent two days in the hospital."

Kendall's gaze drifted to the floor as she quieted.

"What are you thinking about?"

"After I got better, I was pretty out of it." She glanced up at me. "But you know what? My mind felt clearer, and for the first time in years, I felt a surge of creative energy. I went home and wrote the first half of a short story."

"Do you think your illness had something to do with your creative output?"

"Sounds weird, but I yes, I do."

The insight reminded me of my own experience with psychosomatic illness. While I wouldn't wish sickness on anyone, it had promoted psychological change that led me to the field of psychiatry, to this moment.

Kendall leaned forward in her seat. "What are *you* thinking, Dr.

Bloom?"

I hesitated, unsure whether I should share my experience. But Kendall felt like the kind of person who could smell bullshit a mile away, so I figured I shouldn't hold back. And sometimes, letting a patient see something real can build trust.

"A couple years ago," I said, adjusting my glasses, "I got sick during a stressful time in my life, but I made changes and recovered. Once the symptoms were gone, I experienced what you could call post-traumatic growth. I was even inspired to write an essay about my experience, thinking people could learn from it."

Kendall offered a small smile. "I remember reading about the musician Cat Stevens, who got tuberculosis and spent a year in a TB ward. Before he got sick, he was unhappy with his record company. He said his illness gave him time to escape and solitude to reflect. When he left the ward, he said he felt renewed, like he had a new identity. A year and a half later, he released his three best records."

I turned and stared out the window. Was there some kind of "benefit" to getting physically sick? Clearly, Kendall and I had both changed in some way after our illnesses. Then again, I wondered how many patients never recovered from their illness—no breakthrough, no insights—just more suffering, maybe even death.

"It's interesting, right?" Kendall asked, noticing my silence.

When I checked the clock, the session was over. "Yes, it is."

Chapter Nine

The Bloom Center for Counseling Services opened at the start of July, and a heat wave had come to Boston. Luckily, I had three weeks during the transition where I wasn't seeing patients, so I spent the time indoors with air conditioning, reading and catching up on paperwork. I also thought about Kendall and our conversation about illness and post-traumatic growth. I wondered what actually drives that kind of growth through suffering.

I believed I'd gotten sick because my mind and body needed to slow down, to reflect and reset. Being ill lowered my defenses, making it easier to face difficult material. On a more basic level, I also wondered if sickness could lead to greater self-awareness, since it tends to strip away life's background noise. When we're pulled out of our normal routines and cut off from everyday distractions, we're left with space to examine inner qualities we rarely stop to notice. My illness had also brought me closer to death. That brush with mortality pushed me to commit to a more meaningful direction in my career. Without that fall, the Bloom Center would never have existed.

As I continued moving in, I read stories about people who had suffered from an illness and recovered with a changed view of themselves and life. Some had even experienced creative breakthroughs. Such profound experiences were known by different names—from post-traumatic growth to psychological rebirth—but no matter the name, each led the sufferer to a deeper understanding of themselves, the world, or both.

I was particularly struck by the story of American naturalist and writer

John Muir. At twenty-nine, he was working in a factory when a metal filing shot out of a machine and pierced his eyeball. He spent the next month indoors with bandages over both eyes. With nothing to do but think, Muir's mind wandered to places he'd dreamed of seeing, like Yosemite Valley in California. Once he'd fully recovered, Muir reinvented himself, writing, "God has to nearly kill us sometimes, to teach us lessons." He spent the next few months drifting across America, a chronicle of which he would later publish.

It was remarkable how many famous artists and writers had been disabled by tuberculosis before experiencing creative breakthroughs: English poet John Keats, novelist Franz Kafka, and the Scottish writer Robert Louis Stevenson. Stevenson had actually been crippled by TB, spending countless hours in bed, where he found time to write between bouts of grinding pain. Tuberculosis had also affected Voltaire, Anton Chekhov, Fyodor Dostoevsky, Dante, D. H. Lawrence, and Edgar Allan Poe.

Virginia Woolf, who suffered from unexplained fevers, believed her many physical symptoms influenced her creativity and writing. In her diary, she described stumbling from her sickbed, distressed by how much time she'd lost on the novel she was writing, but also appreciative of the time, because it left her with nothing to do but think. I was especially struck by this passage:

> *How astonishing, when the lights of health go down, the undiscovered countries that are then disclosed, what wastes and deserts of the soul a slight attack of influenza brings to view, what precipices and lawns sprinkled with bright flowers a little rise of temperature reveals.*

All of this made me wonder whether Kendall's creative burst was caused by the illness itself, or from the long stretch of under-stimulation that followed. I didn't know, but I was intrigued and planned to keep exploring the question.

* * *

When Kendall arrived for our first session at the new center, she walked into the lobby, eyes wide with admiration. I led her into my consultation room, which was laid out similarly to my office in Boston, and she sat in the chair across from mine.

"I like what you've done with the place," she said.

Feeling modest, I replied, "It's a nice play to lay my head."

After taking care of the payment, I told her that what she'd shared in our last session about her illness had struck a chord with me, and that I'd been doing some research into the relationship between illness and transformation.

"Spooky," she said. "'A song by Cat Stevens came on the radio on my way here."

"That's quite the coincidence," I noted.

Gazing out the window, Kendall twirled a finger through her thin, black hair. Eventually, she turned back to me. "Okay, this might be crazy, but hear me out?"

"Um, okay." I set my pen down on my notepad.

"We both had these brushes with illness, and something good came from them. We know it's true for some other people, too. So, what if you made a healthy person sick… to get the benefits of suffering?"

That *was* crazy. The thought must've shown on my face.

"I mean it," Kendall insisted. "Give me the flu virus or something mildly toxic. Knock me out for a while. When I recover, maybe I'll have itch to write again."

I frowned. "A few problems with that. For starters, all doctors—psychiatrists included—take the Hippocratic oath—"

"Do no harm?" she interrupted. "C'mon, Doc, if I consent, what's the issue?"

"Doctors don't make healthy people sick. It would be profoundly unethical."

"What does 'healthy' even mean? Plenty of people look and act healthy but are emotional messes. What if making them physically sick could make them emotionally healthy?"

Clearly, she wasn't going to drop the idea. I repeated that it would be unethical, and if she wanted to try it, she would have to find another therapist.

She slouched in her chair and huffed. "This way—talking, analyzing, digging for insights—it all just takes *forever* to get anywhere."

I encouraged Kendall to be patient, trust the process. "In my experience, quick changes tend to either fade, or get abandoned. It's the steady work of therapy that leads to lasting, meaningful change."

She seemed unconvinced, but she didn't bring it up again that session.

Chapter Ten

My intention was to spend our next appointment talking more about Kendall's family, especially the relationship with her father. I wanted to learn more about the circumstances surrounding his death, as I still knew so little about it.

When I entered the lobby to meet her, I stopped short, unable to believe what I was seeing. Kendall was slumped in a wheelchair, her head lowered and eyes barely open. Standing behind her was a woman I'd never met.

I rushed over. "Kendall! What's wrong? What happened to you?"

She lifted her head, wincing. When our eyes met, she delivered a subtle grin. "I . . . I ate . . ." She couldn't finish the sentence.

The other woman introduced herself as Kendall's sister, Eva.

"She texted me last night saying she'd eaten meatloaf," Eva explained. "When I got to her apartment, she was on the kitchen floor, clutching her stomach. I don't know what she was thinking. She knows she's allergic!"

I knew *exactly* what she had been thinking. She'd activated her alpha-gal syndrome in an attempt to carry through with her idea from our last conversation.

I glared at Kendall. "You poisoned yourself?"

Her gaze had already dropped to the floor.

"You could've killed yourself!" I shouted.

Grabbing my arm, Eva led me a few feet away, keeping her voice low. "What on earth could've compelled her to do this?"

I shook my head in frustration. "She thinks triggering her meat allergy might help her have some sort of creative breakthrough."

"That's the dumbest thing I've ever heard."

She glanced at Kendall out of the corner of her eye. "She took a leave of absence from work, and now she wants *you* to take care of her while she's sick."

This was out of line—dangerous, insane. "If anyone found out about this, I could lose my medical license." I headed for the bathroom. "This stops now!"

"Where are you going?" Eva shouted.

"I'm getting Benadryl. It'll help curb her allergic reaction."

"No!"

I spun around to find Kendall's head raised, her eyes glowing with desperation. "I will *not* spend my whole life hoping to follow my dreams. I need to do something with my life. Otherwise, I'll just be a nobody, like my dad."

"Kendall—"

"Please, Dr. Bloom," she pleaded. "I want to do this. Please help."

I shook my head and paced back and forth. "I need to think."

Storming into my consultation room, I tried to take stock of the situation. Here was a patient under my care who'd made herself physically sick, thinking it would increase her creative productivity. I was upset, to say the least.

And yet, I'd be lying if I said I wasn't a little curious. What if Kendall's deliberate sickness *did* lead to some kind of burst of creativity? It could be the revolution Kendall desired, and perhaps an advancement for psychiatry—not to mention for my career.

I took off my glasses and cleaned them anxiously. Why not try something more outside the box? It was why I'd started the center, after all. Replacing my glasses on my nose, I made a decision. I'd oversee the experiment, but there would be conditions.

Stiffening my shoulders, I walked back out to the lobby. "You'll stay in one of the finished rooms in the basement," I told Kendall. "I'll hire a nurse to provide medical attention. That person will monitor your health and check your progress. If your health worsens, or you try to poison yourself again, I'll pull the plug."

Kendall's half-open eyes were once again fixed to the floor, but I knew she'd heard me just fine. A grin stretched wide across her face.

Chapter Eleven

The next morning, I woke up early and went straight to Kendall's room in the basement. Trying not to disturb her, I opened the door quietly and found her sleeping on her side. As I approached the bed, she groaned and rolled over to face me.

I sighed, thinking again how insane this was. I'd stayed up half the night thinking I should call her an ambulance and end this nightmare. But something kept me from picking up the phone. Something about the idea intrigued me. Something about Kendall intrigued me.

"How are you feeling?"

She rubbed her eyes. "Like a grenade went off inside me."

"Can you describe it?"

Her face pinched in pain as she listed her symptoms. "Headache, brain fog, stomach pain, crushing fatigue. My throat and esophagus hurt whenever I breathe." She managed a weak smile. "Struggle bus."

"I'm glad you've retained your sense of humor, at least."

I placed my hand on her forehead. It was hot to the touch. Grabbing a wet cloth from the bathroom, I put it on her forehead to try to break the fever.

"I have patients all day, but I'll stop in from time to time to see how you're doing."

Kendall reached for my hand and squeezed it. "I feel like this is going to lead to something great, Dr. Bloom. Thank you for believing in me."

I nodded stiffly, thinking this experiment probably wouldn't lead to anything useful. Most likely, she'd recover from her sickness with no change in her personality, no "benefits." But if I was wrong, if this experiment worked, maybe it could offer a breakthrough in treating other conditions.

Later in the day, I was saying goodbye to a patient when the faint sound of Kendall wailing drifted up from the basement.

"What was that?" my patient asked.

I rubbed the back of my neck nervously. "Oh, I have a cat in the basement."

"Always pegged you as a dog person, Dr. Bloom."

As soon as the front door closed, I ran downstairs and swung open the door to Kendall's room. She was rolling back and forth in bed, crying out in agony.

"I'm calling an ambulance," I yelled. "We're done here."

"No!" she screamed. "I can handle it. I can do this."

"Look at yourself, Kendall!"

She gritted her teeth and delivered the line, an old chestnut from one of my favorite philosophers in college, which seemed to be driving her. "What doesn't kill me makes me stronger, right?"

Had I really let a cliché become the basis for a medical treatment?

Kendall locked eyes with me. "Don't you want to know if it'll work?"

I shook my head in disbelief, truly at a loss for words.

She lifted her chin toward the chair next to her bed. "Sit with me until I fall asleep."

"Kendall? This is—"

I fell silent. She was right; I did want to see what would happen. She was persuasive, so it was hard to say no to her, but there was more to it than that. I didn't want to say goodbye to her yet. It was unprofessional of me, but I liked having her around. So, I sat in the chair beside her and waited until she fell asleep.

* * *

When I visited Kendall the next morning, she was curled up in the fetal position, holding her side in pain.

I rushed to her bed. "Tell me what's going on."

"I feel woozy, but . . ." She closed her eyes and grimaced. "Can you pass me the . . ." She reached for a bucket at the foot of her bed.

I grabbed the bucket and held it underneath her head. She hovered over it and emptied her stomach.

Over the next few days, I took care of Kendall and interviewed candidates for the nursing position in between seeing patients for therapy. I hired Hugo, a good-natured man in his thirties who'd just graduated from nursing school. Every day, Hugo checked Kendall's vitals and delivered basic medical care, like giving her liquid via an IV.

About two weeks into her illness, Kendall started to regain her appetite. Sometimes, I'd visit her during my lunch hour, and we'd talk as we ate together.

"I think the process is working, Dr. Bloom."

"How so?"

"When I'm sick in bed, all I can do is think, and I've been thinking a lot."

"About what?"

"Family, friends, things I've done, things I haven't done, things I'd like to do. But I've also been thinking about bigger stuff."

"Like what?"

"I get these insights about who I am and how I should live my life."

"Can you give me an example?"

"I've thought about how I live this extremely structured, regimented life. From week to week, nothing really changes. I work nine to five, cycling through the same seven to ten outfits every week, eating the same half-dozen meals, watching the same trash TV every night in the same position on my couch."

I smiled softly, pleased to hear her talk about such things. These kinds of insights led to real progress in therapy. "Say more."

"My whole life revolves around reducing uncertainty at every turn. I plan everything obsessively so I don't have to worry about anything unexpected happening. It's all because I can't stand ambiguity or uncertainty."

Now we were making progress, I thought. Working with Kendall, I'd come to see a repressive streak in her, a rigidity that governed how she lived. This had made her a hardworking and productive employee in her job, but it often meant concealing or even cutting off parts of who she was in the process.

"Have you had any insight into what might be driving your behavior?"

"I don't know. Maybe it has something to do with how I was raised. After my parents divorced, my mom and dad moved around a lot, so I was always being shuffled from one house to another. Maybe I crave structure and stability because I didn't have them in childhood." She looked up at me innocently. "What do you think?"

"That's possible, but may I offer another possibility?"

She nodded.

"What if it's about a need for social conformity? The need to be accepted by your peers. Put another way, perhaps you dread their disapproval?"

"I'm always concerned with keeping up appearances," she agreed. "I try to act like everyone else, so I don't stick out."

"How's that make you feel?"

"Like I can't say or do what I want to do, can't be myself. It's not like I want to quit my job and move to Paris to write novels or something romantic; I like my life and what I do for a living. It's just that, emotionally, I'm bottled up."

Nodding, I kept eye contact but didn't respond. Kendall was churning up valuable stuff; I knew better than to stop the flow of her thoughts while she was on a roll.

She then put her face in her hands and started crying. "I'm pathetic! Always living so carefully, constantly worried about what other people think, so constrained."

I delivered the question that often bore fruit with many of my patients: "What do you want, Kendall?"

She exhaled, fixed her gaze on the wall ahead, and thought.

After a while, she wiped her eyes. Without looking away from the wall, she said, "I envy people who are free-spirited—people who seem to do and say as they please."

I gently placed a hand on her shoulder. "You know how you said you're always so bottled up emotionally?"

She sniffled and nodded.

"Well, don't look now, but you just let out a lot of emotions."

Kendall smiled. "That's progress, I guess."

Chapter Twelve

My sessions with Kendall were going well, and by the third week, she was able to keep food down and color had mostly returned to her face. Spending so much time with her, I realized we were dealing with the kind of self-concept issues many of my younger patients went through: understanding one's identity and finding purpose and meaning in one's life.

As we chipped away at these issues, I thought her illness might actually have accelerated the process of identifying and solving them. Being sick seemed to have lowered her guard, allowing us to explore areas of her emotional life that might have been walled off when she was physically and mentally stable.

It certainly wasn't part of my job description, but I started making meals for Kendall. I'd make smoothies in the morning, Hugo usually handled lunch, and in the evening I'd cook dinner, which she and I would eat together in her room.

We enjoyed each other's company, and started to spend more time together before and after my daily appointments. I did what I could to help speed up the healing process. Remembering that Norman Cousins had watched funny movies to bolster his immune system when he was sick, I picked out comedies for us to watch together at night.

Over time, I realized this unconventional situation was changing how we related to each other. A therapeutic environment was an artificial construction, deliberately so. A patient would come into my consultation room, where we'd talk for fifty minutes, and then return to their regular life. With Kendall, this construct had broken down. Instead of fifty minutes once a week, I was often with her for a few hours a day, and I sometimes provided care beyond my therapeutic responsibilities.

As time went on, I realized we might've started to develop feelings for each other. I first noticed I'd perhaps caught feelings during one of our movie nights. I found myself looking forward to the funny moments in the movie just so I could hear the cute little laughs she tried to stifle with a hand over her mouth.

One evening, Kendall was feeling particularly nauseous, so she asked me stay with her until she fell asleep. Hugo had given her a pill for her nausea before he left, but she still felt miserable. We stayed up for a couple of hours and just talked. When she finally fell asleep, I thought about how fully dependent on others she was in this state, like a small child. Her personality had softened, too. When she was healthy, she could be cold and distant, but when she was sick, she was softer, more tender. To my surprise, I liked taking care of her. I wanted to make her feel better and see that she'd be okay.

That night, I passed out in the chair next to her bed. I woke to a soft touch on the back of my hand. Opening my eyes, I took in the strain in her face and asked her what was wrong.

"I don't feel very good, doc."

Glancing at the clock, I saw that it was still early. Hugo wouldn't arrive for several hours, and I didn't have any medicine to give her. "What can I do?"

She reached out a hand. Without thinking, I slipped mine into it. She closed her eyes and smiled warmly. Minutes later, she was sound asleep.

As I returned to my room, I realized we'd crossed a boundary. I should've stopped it then, or even referred her to someone else, but I didn't want to stop seeing her. I cared for her and wanted to be around her as much as I could.

* * *

A week later, Kendall told me she felt nearly healed. Having been confined to a bed for over a month, she wanted to go outside. I thought it was a good idea, so Hugo and I got her out of bed and helped her down the stairs.

Outside, Kendall said she wanted to visit the garden. When we got there, she looked around, watching bumblebees dart between sunflowers. She closed her eyes, took a deep breath, then turned to me and whispered, "Calvin?"

"Yes?" It felt good to hear her use my first name rather than my title.

"Do you have a computer I could use?"

I led her to my spare office, where I set up a laptop for her to use.

Over the next three days, Kendall stayed in that room. She didn't leave to change clothes or shower. A few times a day, I'd knock on the door to check on her or deliver some food, but otherwise, she didn't want to be interrupted.

Whenever I approached the room, I'd hear fingers vigorously tapping keys. I had no idea what she was working on, but I could only imagine it was something she'd been wanting to write for a long time. It surprised me, but it seemed like her illness had, in fact, led to a burst of motivation and creativity.

One morning, Kendall emerged from the room looking like a stray cat but buzzing with giddiness. When she saw me, she ran over and wrapped her arms around me. "I did it, Cal! I finally did it."

I squeezed her tightly; she felt good in my arms. But I didn't know what she was talking about. "What did you do?"

"I finally wrote something of my own!"

"That great! What is it?"

"A long personal essay about how corporate life led me to being creatively blocked, but then I came here, got sick, and recovered with a new zest for life."

She brushed her disheveled hair from her face and shook my shoulders. "It's about what we did here! What we should *continue* to do together."

"I'm happy you're so excited, but what do you mean, 'continue'?"

Her green eyes were wild with excitement. "While I was sick, I had this powerful insight. What if we exposed more people to the benefits of illness? What if we did this program with more people?"

I scanned her face, hoping she wasn't serious. I was just getting over my relief that she hadn't died under my care. Now she wanted to create an experimental program?

"Kendall, I'm a psychiatrist, not a self-help guru running a wellness retreat."

She took hold of my hands. "Calvin, look at me. Really look! I feel so good, healthy. More people need to experience this. More people need to feel how I feel!"

"How could we possibly guarantee that others would have the same experience?"

"I know you know what I mean. You came back stronger after your own illness."

I ran my hand over my beard. "Yes, but that's only two people—"

"You started this center because you wanted to help patients in ways that mainstream therapy couldn't, right? You wanted to offer treatments that would help people with few options left. This could be the start of something revolutionary."

"I run a full-time therapy practice. I don't have time to monitor sick patients."

Kendall called out to Hugo. When he entered the room, she wrapped her arm around him playfully. "Hugo can look after the new patients while you see your regular patients. Isn't that right, Hugo?"

Hugo shrugged. "If it comes with a raise, sure."

"You keep saying 'we.'" I met her eyes. "Are you saying *you* want to be part of this?"

"Yes! Now that I'm recovered I want to stay and help run this program. I'll leave my job at the hospital and handle public relations and marketing for the center. We can make up a title—communications director, whatever. How does that sound?"

"I don't know, Kendall. I'm not sure you fully appreciate what kind of undertaking that would be. Plus, you seem a bit, well, manic. Sometimes, when people come out of a traumatic experience they display this kind of mania—"

"This *isn't* pink cloud. I've had a profound insight, Calvin—a great realization born from the suffering I experienced when I was ill. It's the gift of pain."

"Huh?"

"That's the title of the essay I wrote: 'The Gift of Pain.'"

Chapter Thirteen

I hadn't even agreed to Kendall's proposal before she told her boss she wouldn't be returning to the hospital. That same day, she made my spare office her own space and began handling the center's communications. I still wasn't crazy about her trying to replicate her experience, but I had to admit I liked having her around. I enjoyed her company, and her comms expertise didn't hurt. It'd taken me a week just to write my website's About section.

On a whim, Kendall pitched her personal essay to a few literary publications. An editor at *Memoir Magazine* agreed to publish her story. Not long after it went live, the editor informed her that the piece had officially gone viral with over one hundred thousand likes and shares in the first two days.

By the end of the week, the Bloom Center was flooded with emails and phone calls from people who desperately wanted to do what Kendall had done. I found the public's response worrying. In the eyes of the medical community, what we had done was borderline unethical. I feared a regulatory body might come looking for my medical license if Kendall's story became more widely known. I also suspected it'd be difficult to reproduce her experience, so I didn't want the public to think her outcome would happen for everyone.

One night during dinner, she told me about the emails she'd been getting from people just as repressed and miserable as she'd been.

"There are so many people who feel like they're not getting the help they need. Don't we have an obligation to help them?"

I wanted to remind Kendall that not every reader had gushed over her essay. Some readers who'd lived with chronic illness for years called her "manifesto" toxic positivity. Others claimed she was lying. Kendall, though, was good at brushing off the haters, saying they were just jealous that she'd managed to improve her life without years of therapy.

Shaking my head, I cut a piece of salmon. "Can we just enjoy our dinner—"

"If people consent, it's not unethical, right? People consent to all sorts of crazy stuff—sweat lodges, rituals with hallucinogenic drugs, sensory-deprivation tanks. What's the difference between those and our approach?"

"What if something went seriously wrong?" I blurted out. "What if someone got sicker than we could handle? What if someone *died* under my care?"

"We can retain legal counsel. I know lawyers who can help us draft a consent form and defend us if anything goes wrong."

Kendall had an answer for each of my objections, except for my lack of time. "I'm already stretched thin with my practice."

"I can run the new program while you focus on your regular patients."

She was tenacious, impetuous. I admired that about her, but her refusal to take no for an answer was also angering. Then again, what if she were right? What if this was just the kind of radical program the world needed now more than ever? She'd been right about her situation even though I'd dragged my feet the whole way.

I set down my fork and knife. I almost couldn't believe what I said next. "If we did this, it'd have to be out of the public eye. No news stories about profound recoveries. No patient testimonials. No advertising on our website."

"Deal." Kendall's face brightened. "So, we're doing this?"

I exhaled heavily. "Yes, let's try it."

After a little brainstorming (and a little wine), we named the program "Project Breakthrough," based on the idea that a physical or psychological breakdown could open the door to an emotional, spiritual, or creative breakthrough.

Out of an abundance of caution, I decided to start a pilot program with five select patients. To choose them, I created an intake questionnaire to gather important medical information from prospective candidates. Kendall sent the questionnaire to the sixty people who'd contacted the center to express interest in replicating her experience.

Reviewing the patients' forms, I immediately eliminated about half of the applicants, as they were simply too mentally unwell to take part in the program. It was neither safe nor appropriate to accept patients who were suicidal or dealing with severe mental illness, like schizophrenia or borderline personality disorder.

Once I'd selected the five people, the trickiest part of Project Breakthrough revealed itself. How exactly would we make the patients sick? I started making a list of drugs and medications I knew would sicken someone enough to suffer, but not too ill as to require advanced medical care.

The solution came to us one Saturday morning while we sat in Adirondack chairs on the center's front porch discussing the problem.

"Why not personalize the treatment to each patient?" Kendall asked.

"How do you mean?"

"Eating meat was the perfect way to make me sick because I'm allergic. Why not just exploit an underlying vulnerability in each patient?"

It was brilliant. I already had each patient's medical history and list of preexisting conditions from the intake questionnaire.

Before inviting the patients to the Bloom Center, Kendall and I interviewed them via virtual meetings. Our first call was with a lean, athletic man named Chase, who had a chiseled jawline and blue eyes. He was a creative director, but he wanted to do something different with his life. He just wasn't sure what that would be.

I zeroed in on an early infection he'd indicated on his questionnaire.

"I understand you were infected with the Epstein-Barr virus?"

"I got it at summer camp in high school," Chase replied. "They call mononucleosis the 'kissing disease,' which is hilarious, because I did zero kissing that summer."

I asked how the infection had affected him when he was young.

"I was super tired for a few weeks. I felt better a month after the infection, but I couldn't attend football training camp because my doctor said my spleen could pop."

"As I'm sure you know, the virus stays dormant in your system for life."

"Oh, I know. If I exercise too hard or overwork myself, I pay a high price."

"How so?" Kendall asked.

"I'll be bone-crushingly tired the day after."

I explained to Kendall that some people with the Epstein-Barr virus can develop a chronic form of mononucleosis, which can manifest as chronic fatigue syndrome.

She turned back to Chase. "Would you consent to us inducing your mono?"

Chase nodded. "Have me exercise hard on a stationary bike for about an hour, and the next few days will be hell."

With the course of treatment settled, I turned the conversation to another important detail. "Chase, before we invite you to the center, I'd love to get a better sense of what's drawing you to the program."

He fiddled with a button on his shirt. "I turned forty last year and became seriously depressed, like can't-get-out-of-bed sad."

"Do you have a sense of what caused your depression?"

"I've worked in marketing for twenty years. I like that I get to be creative, but there are too many meetings, too much bureaucracy. At the end of the day, I'm just using all my brainpower to sell consumer electronics."

Kendall leaned closer to the computer screen. "How do you think Project Breakthrough will help?"

"I like the premise: break down to break through, like you wrote in your essay. I feel like I have an entirely different person hiding inside me who I've never given much attention to. I'd like to meet this person. If I don't, I feel like I'm headed for a nervous breakdown. So, why not have that breakdown in a controlled setting with you two wonderful people?"

Kendall smiled and told Chase we'd be able to help him get in touch with his other self. I liked seeing her interact with him. In her professional work, she was often strategic and cerebral, but with patients, she presented a caring, more compassionate disposition. I found this side of her personality endearing, attractive.

We enrolled Chase as our first patient.

For those patients who didn't have exploitable preexisting conditions like Chase, I had to get creative. Eventually, I had a list of a half-dozen drugs that were toxic enough to make someone sick, but not toxic enough to cause serious harm.

"Knock 'em down, not out," Kendall quipped.

The next day, we had another video call with a prospective patient. Annette was an executive director at a nonprofit. Like Chase, she felt like she needed a change. Unlike Chase, however, she loved her work. She was struggling with her marriage.

On the call, Annette wore a tailored blazer, and her chestnut hair was swept up in a bun, framing intelligent eyes and a warm smile. While discussing possible treatment options, Annette suggested infecting her with norovirus. She'd once caught the virus on a cruise, and though the vomiting and diarrhea had saved her from karaoke, she'd ended up spending the entire trip in bed.

Remarkably, Kendall found a way to buy norovirus online and had a few dozen doses shipped to the center. She also found a way to buy *Salmonella*, in case we needed it. She suggested buying stronger chemicals, like mercury or even a chemotherapy agent, but I argued that they were far too potent and could potentially do serious damage.

Before we got off the call, Kendall asked Annette how she thought the program would work for her. Her answer was insightful:

> *Modern society has done a good job of insulating us from adversity, but I've always thought challenge is how we figure out who we are. I'm healthy, I like my job, and I believe in growth through difficulty. I've run a bunch of marathons. Each tested my body and my mind, but they also made me feel capable, accomplished. I'm good as I am, but I think your program could take me further.*

With that, Annette became Project Breakthrough's second patient.

Chapter Fourteen

Before we welcomed Chase, Annette and the other three patients to the center, I rehired the contractor who had remodeled the center to complete the basement rooms, making them livable. I was reviewing architectural plans with him when Arthur called.

"Art!" I answered enthusiastically. "How's life on the Vineyard?"

"Another day in paradise," he replied. "How's everything at Walden Pond?"

I considered telling him about Project Breakthrough, but I decided not to. I wasn't sure how he'd react, and I wanted to get some data first.

Leaving the basement through the back door, I walked out onto the lawn. "We're just starting to hit our stride, I think. What's going on with you?"

"Keeping busy. I gave a talk at a narrative medicine conference last week."

"Passing on your hard-earned wisdom to younger healthcare workers?"

"Have to keep myself busy in retirement."

"And how's Naomi?"

"She's great. Jogging on the beach as we speak."

"You two live a charmed life," I joked.

"Don't I know it!" He paused briefly, switching gears. "So, listen, Calvin, I'd love to swing by sometime and see what you've built."

I froze. "Absolutely but . . ." I scrambled for an excuse. "Give me a couple more weeks to get organized, and I'll carve out some time to properly show you around."

"Sounds like a plan."

"Give Naomi my best."

"Will do!"

The contractor wrapped up the renovations by the end of the week, and the five patients arrived not long after.

Chase was the first to arrive. Carrying a duffel bag, he sported an effortlessly stylish look of fitted jeans and a vintage band T-shirt. We shook hands and made small talk, while Hugo parked Chase's car in a small lot behind the building.

A few minutes later, Annette pulled up in a rideshare. Walking up to us, wearing a silk blouse and black pants, she grinned widely. "I'm looking for Dr. Frankenstein."

Laughing, I shook her hand. "I'd prefer Dr. Bloom, if you don't mind."

Chase shook her hand. "So, you're the funny one."

"Glad someone likes my humor," Annette replied. "My husband can't stand my jokes."

The other three patients arrived not long after. There was Gavin, whose wrinkled, drab clothing mirrored his dull, lifeless eyes. He'd joined the program because he was "boring" and needed something—anything—to become a more interesting person.

Then there was Abby, an administrator at a liberal arts college in Central Massachusetts. She had a bubbly personality and an infectious laugh, and her eclectic outfit reflected a quirky, outgoing nature.

Finally, there was Jordan, a burnt-out high-school physics teacher who'd been teaching for almost twenty years. He'd expressed a desire to do something "more chill" when he wasn't at school. Ever the academic, he wore khaki trousers and a tweed jacket over a button-down shirt.

Kendall and I gave the group a tour of the building before settling in for a communal dinner. Afterward, we gathered in the garden, and I addressed the group.

"Before we show you to your rooms and let you settle in, I'd like for us to take a little walk in the woods. We want to give you space to truly consider what you've signed up for and an opportunity to leave if it feels too overwhelming."

I led the group onto a narrow trail, which we strolled along for about twenty minutes, until we reached a vista with a 360-degree view of the forest. Stepping to the front of the group, I delivered an official welcome.

"You've all come to the Bloom Center at great personal sacrifice. You've left families, friends, and careers behind. You've put your lives on hold for an indefinite period of time to take part in an experiment to better yourselves. Before your journey begins, we've brought you to this beautiful location to say a few words."

I swiveled my head to gaze out across the treetops.

"Why is suffering necessary to living a good life?" I asked rhetorically. "In the 1980s, scientists created Biosphere 2, the world's largest enclosed ecological system, to explore the viability of supporting life on another planet. The three-acre structure had a variety of small environments, including a rainforest, a coral-reef ocean, and a savannah."

I nodded at Kendall, who smiled and picked up where I left off. "During the experiment, scientists were confused to find that trees inside Biosphere 2 weren't maturing, eventually falling over and dying." Her eyes flitted across the group. "Why do you think this happened? Why might the trees have failed to thrive?"

"Maybe the soil didn't have the right nutrients?" Chase tried.

"Good guess," Kendall said, "but the problem wasn't the soil."

"Did it involve the irrigation system?" Annette asked. "Maybe the trees weren't getting enough water."

"That's not it either."

Gavin chimed in. "Aren't these types of issues usually human error? Someone must've screwed up somewhere."

Kendall shook her head and offered a hint to the group. "In such an artificial environment, what might be missing?"

Abby, who had been rubbing her chin, jerked her head up. "Wind!"

Kendall beamed. "Exactly! The scientists realized that in order to grow strong, the trees needed *wind*, which these ecological environments lacked."

"But what's so special about wind?" Chase asked with a frown.

I took over the explanation. "Wind strengthens a tree's root system by causing it to grow 'stress wood,' which gives trees their integrity and strength. Similarly, if we live stress-free lives and don't experience any hardship or adversity, we, too, can become weak and vulnerable. Just like wind makes for strong trees, adversity and struggle drive the healthy development of humans."

The patients nodded and murmured in agreement.

"Project Breakthrough offers an opportunity for you to experience suffering within a controlled medical setting. This will give you time to introspect, reflect, perhaps rework the egos you've spent your whole lives carefully constructing."

As the sun set, we strolled back to the center. Kendall and I followed behind as the patients chatted with one another. Leaning in close, she playfully bumped her hip into mine and wrapped her arm around my waist. I pulled her close against my side. I liked the way we fit together, the way she smelled, the way she looked up at me with affectionate eyes.

I had a crush on her. I figured she probably did, too.

"I can't believe we're really doing it, Calvin."

"Crazy, right? It's a bit scary, though. So many unknowns."

"Less scary when we're doing it together."

"Misery loves company," I quipped.

Entering the center through the front door, we paused in the lobby, where Hugo stood with his hands clasped behind his back. Catching the attention of our patients, I indicated the Bloom Center's nurse. "Hugo will escort you to your rooms, where you'll receive your individual therapies soon."

Chase raised his hand. "When will we start feeling . . . sick, Dr. Bloom?"

"Each therapy is personalized, so the onset of symptoms will differ from person to person. However, it's likely you'll start feeling ill within a day or two."

Kendall spoke up reassuringly. "We'll be with you every step of the way. If anything goes wrong, Dr. Bloom or Hugo can provide expert medical care."

"You were the first to go through this experience," Annette said to Kendall. "Any advice for us?"

Kendall pulled up one of her shirtsleeves to reveal a tattoo I'd never seen before that read: *The obstacle is the way.*

"When things got tough during my illness journey, these words gave me comfort. My advice? Lean into the pain, surrender to the suffering, and keep in mind that your sickness isn't permanent. It will pass." Turning, she smiled at me. "Trust the process."

Gavin cleared his throat. "What if we decide we don't want to be here anymore?"

This was a possibility Kendall and I had prepared for. "If at any time you'd like to stop treatment," I said, "just use the safe word *Walden*. We'll get you home right away."

Gavin seemed satisfied, so I nodded to Hugo to lead everyone to their rooms.

"Wait!" Hugo exclaimed, raising a finger.

"What is it, Hugo?" I asked.

Instead of answering, he jogged to his office and returned with a small bell. Approaching Chase, Hugo offered him the accompanying striker. "To signify the beginning of your journey."

Chase squinted at Hugo but obliged him, striking the bell. It produced a high-pitched chime. Smiling, Chase handed the striker to Annette.

Hugo held the bell as each patient took a turn ringing it.

Standing back, I watched everyone participate in the ritual. It might not have been scientific, but I understood that the gesture symbolized the start of our patients' path forward and fostered a sense of camaraderie between them.

As the bell fell silent after the final strike, I blurted out, "May you have a meaningful journey." I wasn't sure what had prompted the words, but the patients all murmured their thanks before following Hugo down into the basement.

Kendall closed the basement door behind the last patient and blew out a heavy breath. Pulling out her phone, she checked the time. "Shoot, it's late. I hate driving home in the dark." She glanced at me. "I don't suppose you have a place I could stay here."

"Take the guest room. It's all made up."

Grinning slyly, she strutted toward me. "And how much does it cost to stay in the good doctor's room?"

Kendall wasn't trying to hide her interest, and the prospect of making our relationship more intimate stirred my arousal. I tried to play it cool, though. "It's quite pricey right now. Peak season, you know?"

"Hmm." She bit her lip teasingly. "Maybe I could get an employee discount?"

Closing the distance between us, I laid my hands on her hips. "I could knock thirty percent off the retail price."

Kendall shifted closer, until her face was only inches from mine, her gaze locked on my lips. "I was thinking more like half off. I'm a vital team member, Dr. Bloom."

I wanted so badly to kiss her, but the sexual tension building between us was intoxicating. Rubbing her lower back, I smiled.

"Let's meet in the middle, then. Forty percent?"

"Deal." Kendall pulled me in and pressed her lips to mine.

We kissed right there in the lobby. Occasionally, she pulled back to let the passion build further before resuming.

I knew what she wanted; I wanted it too.

Finally, Kendall broke away, grabbed my hand, and led me upstairs.

Chapter Fifteen

It had been three weeks since Kendall and I first spent the night together, and she'd been sleeping over most nights since. One morning, I woke to sunlight and soft snoring. Rolling over, I admired the curves of Kendall's body—her shapely legs, strong lower back—and the way her long black hair spilled across her olive-colored skin. Scooting closer, I pressed my body into hers and wrapped an arm around her. Stirring, she moaned and wiggled her backside into me. We laid there for a while, all tangled up, warm and cozy, drifting in and out of consciousness.

I couldn't have been happier. I'd had my share of lukewarm relationships over the years, ones I'd been fairly certain from the beginning wouldn't last beyond the honeymoon phase but being with Kendall felt different, like it could last. There was also something special about starting a new relationship just as Project Breakthrough began.

But I also worried. Entering a relationship with her would complicate things. I'd had a relationship with a woman I worked with once before, and when it had ended, working together became awkward.

We lingered in bed for a while before wandering into the kitchen for breakfast. As I made smoothies, she prepared coffee. Once it was ready, she held out a mug of coffee for me to take. Before I could grab it, she tapped a finger against her lips. "The cost of coffee."

I kissed her softly. "Small price to pay."

We took our breakfast out on the second-floor deck overlooking the woods. It was a lovely fall morning. The temperature was in the high sixties, and there was no humidity.

Kendall took the first sip of her smoothie and lifted the jar to inspect its contents. "I'm sorry?" she teased. "Did Chef Ramsay make this smoothie?"

"You didn't know? The Bloom Center offers a two-star Michelin restaurant."

She nodded playfully. "I'll update the website by end of day."

We sat out on the deck for an hour, enjoying our breakfast as we listened to the rise and fall of cicadas, the chirps of crickets, and the melody of birdsong. The forest's symphony was the best music.

Occasionally, I'd steal a glance at Kendall. When she caught me looking, she smirked and blew me a kiss.

As we sat there in silence, my mind drifted to Project Breakthrough.

"What are you thinking about over there, Dr. Bloom?" she asked.

"I'm starting to wonder if your breakthrough might've been an anomaly."

"What makes you say that?"

"It's been three weeks, and we're still not seeing results. We had to induce a second crash for Chase when he didn't show positive growth after his first bout of illness. And we're planning to reinfect Annette with norovirus if we don't see any noticeable changes in her personality."

"It's still too early to judge the program's success," Kendall insisted. "I was in bed for a month after triggering my meat allergy." Walking over, she rubbed my back. "The good doctor here saw me through my illness. When I recovered, I had my breakthrough. They will too."

"And what if our patients don't respond like you did?"

"Just because we're having trouble replicating my experience, doesn't mean we've failed. We're still fine-tuning our treatments and procedures."

"All we have right now is a handful of very sick people in our basement."

"It'll work." She winked at me. "Trust the process."

My mind was swirling with thoughts when the right side of my head began to throb. I pinched my nose, trying to dull the pain. A bad headache was coming, and I needed to lie down before I got too nauseous.

"Are you okay?" she asked.

Nodding, I made up a reason to excuse myself. Kendall narrowed her eyes in concern but didn't press further.

As I got up from my chair, my left ring finger started twitching, and she noticed. "What's up with that crazy finger of yours?"

I shoved my hand into my pocket. "Forgot to take my B vitamins."

She rubbed the back of my head. "Maybe you should take it easy before your first patient gets here. You look a bit tense."

"That's a good idea."

I was walking upstairs to lie down when I heard a muffled sound coming from the basement. "You hear that?" I asked Kendall.

She nodded. "Sounds like . . . crying."

"Or yelling." I changed directions and jogged to the basement door, Kendall right behind me. The wailing grew louder as we descended down the stairs. Following the sound, I ran down the hallway to Chase's room. When I entered, I saw Annette kneeling at the foot of Chase's bed, holding his hand. Her reddish-brown hair, usually secured up in a bun, flowed freely around her shoulders.

"What's going on?" I asked, breathing heavily.

"I'm just keeping him company," Annette replied. "He's really going through it."

As Chase's face contorted in pain, Annette wiped sweat from his forehead.

Kendall ran into the room. "Is everything alright? Who—"

"All good." I raised my hand. "Annette's taking care of Chase."

"Oh." Kendall smiled. "That's sweet."

It was, actually. I liked seeing one patient helping another, but more than that, I'd seen the way Chase and Annette had been interacting. A friendship was growing between them, perhaps more.

"Well, carry on," I said, seeing no reason to stay any longer.

Suddenly, Annette pressed a hand to her stomach and stood up fast. "Actually, could one of you take over for a bit?"

"Of course," I replied. "Something wrong?"

Annette passed me, gripping her stomach. "Nature calls."

Chapter Sixteen

Crawling out of bed the next morning, I went to the bathroom and looked at myself in the mirror. A weary man stared back. My skin was pale, a stark contrast to the dark circles under my eyes. I threw back three pills for the migraine that still lingered.

I tried not to wake Kendall as I slipped back into bed, but she stirred, rolled over, and nuzzled her head into my neck. I loved our mornings, holding each other as we fell in and out of sleep.

As I drifted off, my thoughts turned to memories of taking care of her when she was sick: The long nights spent trying to break a fever; holding her hair back as she hunched over the toilet; laughing hysterically during movie nights. The more time I spent with her, the more her mental and physical health had improved. This made me think about how Arthur had given Naomi extra care when they first met and how Annette was tending to Chase through his toughest days.

Just then, I was struck by a revelation. Could warmth, companionship, affection—dare I say, *love*—be the medicine our patients needed to have the breakthroughs they so desperately wanted?

I jumped out of bed and threw on sweatpants.

Kendall rolled over and peered up at me. "What's going on?"

"I think I know why our program isn't working, why the patients aren't responding."

Kendall sat up, her face bright with curiosity. "Say more."

"What's the difference between your illness journey and our patients'?"

She thought for a moment. "I don't know."

"I took care of you while you were sick. I didn't just provide medical care; I comforted you. You had someone to talk to, a shoulder to cry on when things got tough. See the difference?"

Her eyes widened. "That's what Project Breakthrough's missing!"

I raced downstairs, excited to put this new idea into action. Visiting each room in the basement, I explained my plan to each patient. "If you want to talk, we can talk," I told Chase. "If you want to play a game, we can play a game," I said to Annette. "If you'd rather keep to yourselves for a bit, that's fine," I told Gavin, Abby, and Jordan.

Over the next week, I developed a daily routine of visiting each patient at least once to talk with them, listen to them, or laugh with them. Working with Hugo and Kendall, we did whatever we could do to brighten our patients' days. We put fresh flowers in their rooms, brought them books, shared baked goods and fresh fruit.

We even wrote emails for them or jotted down ideas and recorded thoughts while they talked aloud. When a patient was really sick, one of us would just sit at their bedside and provide space for them to suffer through their discomfort, sometimes holding their hand, or rubbing their head, always providing some comforting words.

Before long, we'd turned the previously sterile-looking basement into a comfortable, lived-in space. "A home within a hospital," I liked to say. Hugo set up a smart speaker in the common area that played calming music, and Kendall lit pine-scented candles that made the space smell like a forest. The patients loved her "wild tea," which she made from needles of evergreen trees in the woods, and was filled with vitamin C.

With their permission, we made changes to each patient's diet. We avoided foods containing refined sugar, or processed products, and kept them away from simple starches, like white bread. The meals we cooked for them consisted of mostly organic food and copious amounts of vegetables and fruit. Everyone's favorite meal was a vegetable medley with tofu and a variety of spices.

The highlight of most days was when we wheeled our patients out onto the building's wraparound porch so they could enjoy the fresh New England air. We'd help them onto the Adirondack chairs lined up along the porch and wrap them in blankets to keep them warm. Despite often feeling miserable, they'd lounge in the chairs and share stories, laughing together, sometimes crying together.

One day, I went out to check on everyone between my regular patients and found Gavin, Jordan, and Abby playing a game of Monopoly.

"Who's winning?" I asked.

Gavin pushed his unkempt hair off the side of his face. "Abby's dominating."

"As per usual," Abby replied, as she studied the board.

Jordan adjusted his rectangular glasses. "This game's far from over."

She rolled her eyes. "A man should know when he's beat."

I surveyed the board to see that Abby was, indeed, in a dominant position. She'd purchased hotels on the most valuable areas and seemed to still have a lot of money too.

"I'm afraid she might be right, Jordan," I said.

He grimaced. "I should've stayed in bed today."

I looked around the porch. "Where are Chase and Annette?"

"You mean the love birds?" Gavin scoffed. "I think they're in Chase's room, reading poetry to each other or something lame like that."

"If I have to hear her talk about Chase's 'baby-blue eyes' one more time"—Jordan stuck a finger in his mouth, pretending to gag—"I'll throw myself off this deck."

Abby punched Jordan in the arm. "I think it's cute."

Gavin socked Jordan in the other arm. "You're just jealous."

Jordan smirked at me. "I can't tell what's making me sick: the medication or them."

I chuckled. "Just say *Walden*, and it can all come to an end."

Jordan huffed. "And go back to the classroom? Where kids stare at their phones while I try to get them to learn Newton's Laws of Motion? No thanks, I'll stay here and get my butt kicked in Monopoly."

"You just love us, admit it!" Abby shouted.

Jordan tossed the dice across the board. "Don't get too comfortable; I can still beat you."

Abby directed her sarcasm at me. "Keep an eye on Jordan, doc, I think he might be experiencing a break from reality."

Shaking my head, I laughed and strolled off to prep for my next patient.

Back in my office, I thought about how our patients seemed almost like teenagers at summer camp—chilling, cracking jokes, even developing crushes. They were having the best time here. What an unexpected and wonderful outcome.

We continued adding activities we thought might help lift our patients' spirits as they struggled. If patients felt they could handle some light exercise, I'd bring in a yoga teacher to teach a class on the front lawn. Kendall and I usually took advantage of the yoga classes ourselves. They were a relaxing break from our daily obligations.

During class, the teacher would ask us to feel the energy moving through our bodies as we moved in sync. I'd always feel a warm energy travel from my hands through my core and into my feet. Kendall and I would occasionally steal glances at each other as we moved through positions, and at the end of class, lying side by side, she always reached over to hold my hand. It was the best feeling.

Chapter Seventeen

After a couple weeks of giving our patients extra care, we started seeing positive changes. Even though they were still technically sick from the therapies we'd given them, they reported "suffering less" when we were more present and comforting. According to our records, they also had fewer complaints and needed less pain medication.

Our most cherished routine was movie nights on Tuesdays and Thursdays. On one particular Thursday evening, Kendall, Hugo, and I helped Chase, Annette, Gavin, Abby, and Jordan out of their beds and up to the first floor, where we settled them into chairs and couches in the living room.

Kendall tucked a blanket around Chase, who was still pale and shivering after the previous night's intense workout. "You sure you don't want to go back to bed?"

"This'll be good distraction," Chase replied, pulling the blanket to his chin. "What's that tattoo of yours say again? 'The obstacle is the way'?"

She nodded. "You're a trooper."

"He sure is," Annette whispered from the seat next to him.

Chase smiled. "If you feel like puking, Annette, please turn left, not right."

"But you'd look so cute covered in my vomit," she shot back.

Everyone started laughing. It was gallows humor, the kind Arthur said had carried him through the brutal slog of med school.

Using the remote, I scrolled through movies on a streaming platform.

"So many options," Abby said as she reclined in her chair. "So little time."

Jordan coughed into his hand. "All we have is time, Abbs."

"You don't look so hot, Jordan," Abby said. "You *sure* you have that much time?"

"Okay, okay, settle down, crew," I interjected. "What do we want to watch?"

"Something funny," Gavin said, "but darkly funny, like weird or ironic."

"I second that!" Abby said.

Nodding, I began scrolling through the horror-comedy genre.

"Stop," Gavin shouted after a moment. "Go back."

Scrolling back, I stopped on *Irrational Man*, a movie starring Joaquin Phoenix as a philosophy professor. The description read, "Plagued by depression and existential despair, Abe Lucas finds renewed purpose through a sinister act of poisoning."

"Push play!" Abby yelled.

In unison, the group chanted, "Play, play, play—"

"Okay!" I started the film.

I switched off the lights and made my way to the couch where Kendall lay sprawled beneath a blanket. "Room for me?"

She smiled and lifted the blanket so I could climb underneath. I situated myself behind her, big spoon to her little spoon.

She groaned with delight. "So comfy cozy."

As the movie started, I glanced around. It felt like we were all part of one big, crazy family or fraternity, all in on this wild ride together, unsure how it'd turn out, but it seemed to be working well enough so far.

We all seemed to enjoy watching the movie's dark premise play out. The professor, Abe, was struggling with a sense of meaninglessness. In one scene, he overhears a woman talking about an unethical judge, who was jeopardizing her custody battle. Believing that carrying out vigilante justice would give his life meaning, Abe decides to murder the judge with cyanide, which he steals from his college's chemistry lab.

"Cyanide," Kendall muttered. "Maybe we should get our hands on some of that?"

"Um, no," I replied. "We're trying to sicken, not kill."

She slapped my arm. "I was just kidding."

"Were you?" I whispered.

She turned away, her attention already back on the screen.

As the movie went on, we saw how the act of poisoning seemed to reinvigorate Abe, giving him a fresh sense of purpose. However, as I suspected, the murder ultimately led to his downfall, as suspicions arose and his crime unraveled, culminating in his accidental death as he tried to cover up his crime.

After the movie ended, we spent a few minutes sharing our thoughts. Seeing that it was getting late, I told the group it was time for bed. Kendall, Hugo, and I helped everyone into the basement and back to their rooms.

Once everyone was settled, Kendall and I headed upstairs. She hopped into bed and rolled over to face me. As I clicked off the light, she brought up the idea of using cyanide again. "What if we used just a tiny amount? It could—"

"Who has a medical license here?" I said, wanting to end the conversation.

"You're such a wimp sometimes, you know that?"

I climbed into bed and scooted close to her. "And you're nuts."

She pulled my face toward hers. "Yeah, well, you like the crazy ones." She ran her fingers through my hair and kissed me.

month into changing our program's approach to healing, Chase had recovered from a bout of illness and said he was ready to go home. Before graduating him from the program, Kendall insisted on conducting an interview with him to gather feedback. Attending the interview, I finally began to fully grasp the power of Project Breakthrough.

Kendall pressed the record button on a tape recorder before turning to Chase. "How has this experience changed you?"

"I feel like I'm seeing things clearly for the first time," he replied.

"How so?"

"For most of my life, I've relied on the analytical part of my brain. But when I was sick, I started listening to my intuition."

"And what did your intuition tell you?"

"To leave marketing and never look back!" he said without flinching. "I'm quitting my job the second I get home."

"Did you think about what you might want to do now?"

"I've always felt like I should've been a social scientist. I've learned a lot in marketing that I can apply to a career change to, say, anthropology, like conducting quantitative and qualitative research and leading focus groups."

"What do you find appealing about social sciences?"

"Anthropology is about gaining knowledge, not making a profit." He hesitated. "I've never said this out loud, but I don't really care about money."

Just like that, Chase went home, intending to change careers.

A few days later, Annette graduated, following in Chase's footsteps. In her interview, she admitted she'd married her husband for the wrong reasons and was set on filing for divorce once she got home. Around the center, the gossip was that she and Chase wouldn't wait long to start dating.

While Chase and Annette felt that removing certain stressors from their lives—a job, a relationship—would clear space for something better, Jordan and Abby realized they could improve their lives by *adding* things. Jordan said he wanted to cook more, maybe even buy a food truck. Abby talked about wanting to make films.

Gavin said he was still bored but seemed relieved to have a break from his usual routine. "I realized I don't have any joy in my life," he told us in his exit interview. "I was thinking about picking up a hobby."

"What kind of hobby?" Kendall asked.

"I always thought archery was cool."

It became clear that the suffering our patients experienced had, in fact, given them time to look inward and reflect on unexplored parts of themselves.

My favorite review of Project Breakthrough came from Annette, whose experience reminded her of the song "Live Like You Were Dying" by Tim McGraw. In her written feedback, which was required of every patient before leaving, she wrote:

> *I used to think this song was lame, but having been sick to the point of feeling like I could die, I get it now. Being in bed for six weeks, I examined my regrets. I should've asked the guy I liked to dance at my high school prom. I should've studied abroad in Switzerland. I should've left my husband the first time he cheated. It's true what Kendall wrote in her essay: illness can be a teacher, a gift, an opportunity to step back and look at yourself and your life differently.*

I couldn't have been happier for everyone, and I truly hoped future patients would have similarly positive outcomes.

Later that evening, Kendall and I were preparing dinner when I glanced at her and felt overcome by desire. Walking over to her, I put my arms around her waist and rocked back and forth playfully.

"Excuse me," she teased, "you're violating my personal space."

I planted soft kisses on her neck. "And if I don't stop?"

She reached for some parsley and started slicing it as I moved around her neck. "Did you know that, in large quantities, parsley is poisonous to humans?"

I thought of the movie we'd just watched and chuckled. "You wouldn't poison a man you love, would you?"

Setting the knife down, she turned to face me. "Love, hm?"

I shrugged. "Yeah, I love you, Kendall."

She hugged me and whispered in my ear, "Love you too, baby." She gave my cheek a peck and went back to cutting.

I opened a bottle of red wine and shook my head. "I can't believe Project Breakthrough's working. It's *really* working."

"It's so exciting. We need to go through the new applications."

I handed Kendall a glass of wine. "Let's get into it tomorrow."

She took a sip from the glass. "I know one of the conditions you had for starting the program was that patients shouldn't share their experiences with the press. I think we should ask our patients to sign NDAs."

I said it was a good idea, and she said she'd start working on a draft in the morning.

"What would I do without you?" I asked.

"You'd be lost." She smiled and tapped her neck with the knife, telling me to keep kissing. "Now back to work, Dr. Bloom."

Chapter Nineteen

Encouraged by the success of our first batch of patients, I couldn't wait to welcome the next group of five individuals, all eager to experience the breakthrough Kendall had dramatized so well in her personal essay. Similar to the first batch, we planned to use different methods to induce illness: triggering allergies, causing foodborne reactions, or giving them a drug that made them unwell.

The first patient to arrive in our second group was a morbidly obese, middle-aged man named Max, who told us his sister had sent him because she was worried about his health. Max confessed that he didn't have much faith in our program. He'd only signed up because his sister had threatened to stop giving him money if he didn't at least try to make a change in his life.

I was showing Max his room when he said, between heavy breaths, that Project Breakthrough probably wouldn't work on him.

Curious to hear his perspective, I asked him to explain why.

"Every night, I eat to the point of sickness. And yet no breakthroughs."

Max was being glib, but he had a point. Eating yourself sick wasn't going to change anything. Wanting to learn more about his eating habits, I asked, "How would you say you eat on a daily basis?"

"I don't eat much during the day, but at night, I go nuts."

"Define nuts."

"I usually order a few meals from the nearest fast-food place, then I wash it all down with a liter of soda, candy bars, chips, and all sorts of other trash."

Max had stopped breathing so heavily, but he still looked exhausted. I wondered when he'd last gotten a good night's sleep.

"Why do you think you eat to the point of sickness?"

He folded his massive body into the chair in the corner of his room. "Because it makes my taste buds light up like a Christmas tree."

"Of course, but you can see how gorging yourself on junk food every night isn't, well, healthy for you?"

Max dropped the jokes. "Well, it doesn't take a psychiatrist to figure it out," he replied. "Clearly, I'm unhappy with my life."

This felt like a start, I thought.

He explained that he didn't have any friends and hadn't had a girlfriend since college. A few years ago, he might have been able to get a job, but his weight kept going up, until he could barely stand long enough to get to the door for his food deliveries. At this point, he was housebound.

"During your time here," I said, "we could explore dietary changes and healthy eating habits. Would you be willing to try some of our suggestions?"

Max seemed to understand that I cared and agreed to try. "I know my eating is out of control. I think it started when I was young. My mom always insisted that my sister and I 'clear our plates,' no matter how much food she served or how awful it tasted."

My phone buzzed in my pocket. It was probably Kendall letting me know that other patients had arrived.

"I'm really glad you're here, Max," I said. "I think we'll be able to make progress with your weight in our program." Scanning the room, I invited him to settle in. "The other patients are arriving. We'll all meet for orientation before treatment starts."

As I was leaving, Max spoke up. I turned back to see his eyes lowered and his lips pressed tightly together. "When is dinner, Dr. Bloom?"

I smiled gently, sensing his embarrassment. As a psychiatrist, I never judged my patients; I accepted them for who they were and just aimed to understand them—to really "see" them—and hopefully help them unearth whatever was troubling them.

"I'll let Hugo know you're hungry. He'll prepare whatever you want."

He looked relieved. "Thanks, Doc."

"You made the right decision coming here, Max."

As I walked away, I wondered whether I actually believed this, or if I was just saying it to comfort Max. I had some doubts about his ability to withstand our program.

* * *

On the way to visit Hugo, I walked past Kendall's office and caught her staring, glassy-eyed, at her computer screen.

"Everything alright?"

"Just a flare of fatigue," she said. "I stupidly had a steak tip last night."

I could tell there was more she wasn't saying. I squinted, urging her to say more.

She exhaled and tilted the screen toward me. It was a Yelp review. The name at the top stopped me. "Gavin?" I said. "Our Gavin?"

She nodded. "Just read."

I skimmed the page. The Bloom Center had all five-star reviews, from our former patients, and even a few people we didn't know. And then there was Gavin's. One star. Sitting there like a bruise. He wrote:

> *We're all exhausted, so it was nice to take a break, but having flu-like symptoms for a couple weeks didn't change my life. I realized in the program that I needed a hobby, so I started archery. Turns out I wasn't any good at it, and I didn't feel like learning how to get better. I met some nice people in Project Breakthrough, but*

it turned out to be a waste of time.

I looked up. Kendall's face was strained.

"Are we doing the right thing?" she asked quietly. "Are we actually helping people? Or is this just wellness retreat for burned-out professionals?"

I'd never seen her like this, questioning the very thing we were building. I tried to be honest, but reassuring. "I'm still not sure. Let's give it time."

She pressed both palms into her temples, then let out a long breath. "I never really liked Gavin. Thought he was weak, not willing to do the work." She paused. "Maybe some people just aren't cut out to suffer their way into a better life."

"Maybe," I said, not knowing what else to say.

* * *

The other patients arrived throughout the day, and we helped them settle into their rooms. I asked Hugo and Kendall into the living room to talk about Max's care.

"Hugo, if you could do a full workup on him, that would be great. Get a baseline of his vitals and keep a close eye on them during treatment."

Hugo took a seat, nodding. "I've already reviewed the medical records he brought with him. I'm somewhat concerned about his heart health."

Kendall tilted her head, looking curious.

I had similar doubts, so I asked him to explain further.

"His blood pressure is outrageously high, and his other numbers—cholesterol, insulin sensitivity, lipid profile—are all off the charts."

Hearing that, I figured Max was probably too sick to be here. And since the second wave hadn't technically started yet, I said what was on my mind. "If we're sending him home, now's the time to decide."

Hugo thought for a moment. "I think he's too much of a liability."

Kendall had been quiet, but she finally spoke up. "Look, we can't just reject someone because they're a difficult case. Now's the best time to work with a patient like Max, someone who's weight is almost certainly the result of unexplored emotional factors that he might uncover during his time here."

It was logical, but I was leaning toward agreeing with Hugo. "I don't know. If something happened to him, we'd be responsible and we could get into a lot of trouble."

Kendall didn't back down. "If Max gained some deep insight into what's driving his eating behavior and weight issues, think about the transformation he'd experience. Think about how that would reflect on our program—on us."

I looked at Hugo, who just lifted his shoulders. "Your call, Dr. Bloom."

I thought for a moment, gnawing on my lip. "It's true that if Max's time here led to that level of insight, it'd be a huge breakthrough for him and perhaps even the field of psychiatry. So, maybe it's worth the risk. Maybe we're the only ones who can help him now. That leads us to the next question: how could we make him sick?"

Hugo leaned forward. "I have an idea."

I nodded, urging him to continue.

"What if we gave him one of the new weight-loss medications, like a GLP-1? We could start him on once-a-week injections of 0.5 mg."

"Whenever he'd try to binge eat," I said, "he'd get unbearably sick. Good idea."

"So he'd just want to eat less all the time?" Kendall asked.

"Most people have really bad nausea when they start a GLP-1," Hugo added.

Kendall sat down and crossed her legs. "Yes, but doesn't prescribing

Max a weight-loss medication defeat the purpose of Project Breakthrough? Wouldn't that just make him lose weight by suppressing his appetite? Seems like a quick fix. This whole program is supposed to be the very *opposite* of a quick fix."

She had a point.

I turned to Hugo with another possibility. "What about giving him Vyvanse?"

"What's that?" Kendall asked.

"Medication approved for the treatment of ADHD, but it's also the only FDA-approved drug to treat binge-eating disorder."

Hugo thought for a moment and then started rattling off side effects that could be useful for our program. "It can mess with people's stomach, make them feel nauseous, even cause vomiting."

"So?" I said.

Hugo shifted in his seat. "It could work."

Kendall leaned back in her chair, looking pleased.

I thought about dosage. For treating binge-eating disorder, a medium dose of Vyvanse was usually within the range of 40 mg to 50 mg per day.

"Start him off at a lower dose, 40 mg once daily," I told Hugo. "Vyvanse is a powerful stimulant, so he might get jittery, have trouble sleeping, feel anxious."

"Copy that," Hugo said.

"Wait." Kendall stood up. "Why start with a low dose?"

Hugo looked frustrated with her, which was a first. "Because that's how medicine works, Kendall. Start low, go up as needed."

"Yes, under normal conditions within a normal setting," Kendall shot back. "But Max is an abnormal patient in a *very* abnormal setting." She turned to me. "Why not start with a higher dose? If he's not getting really sick during the program, what's the point?"

Hugo threw up his hands and just stared at me.

"Fine, start him at 50 mg, but keep a close eye on him."

Hugo stood, avoiding eye contact with Kendall. "I should check on the others."

"Thank you, Hugo."

I didn't have another patient for an hour. I hadn't slept well the night before, and I needed to clear my head. "I'm going for a walk."

Kendall pranced up to me. "You're a genius, you know that?"

"Just doing my job," I joked.

She slapped me on the backside and scampered down the hallway.

Chapter Twenty

Two weekends later, I was writing up notes after a patient visit when I got a call from Arthur. Taking a deep breath, I answered, knowing it was time to tell him about our program. I should have told him weeks ago, but I hadn't known how to start the conversation, perhaps I'd been afraid to tell him what we'd been doing.

Still, I couldn't tell him over the phone; I needed to show him.

After our initial pleasantries, I asked, "Can you visit the center today, Art? There's something I'd like to show you."

He paused before agreeing. "I'll hop on the ferry, be there this afternoon."

A few hours later, I opened the front door to see Arthur standing on the other side. His Hawaiian shirt depicted a whimsical scene of surfers riding electric-purple waves.

I shook his hand heartily. "It's been too long."

Arthur returned the gesture with a strong handshake and then gave me a big bear hug. "Some place you have here, Calvin!"

I waved him in. "Please, come in."

Arthur stepped into the main lobby.

I turned to introduce Kendall who had come to meet the famous Dr. Pratt. "I'd like you to meet Kendall, the Bloom Center's comms director."

They shook hands, and I led a tour, Kendall following closely behind.

As we strolled through the building, Arthur swiveled his head, admiring the architecture and interior design. "Is it true this place used to be an old asylum?"

"Concord Almshouse," I confirmed. "I renovated and downsized it."

We stopped at an office about halfway down the main hallway. "This is where Kendall does her magic," I said. Farther down the hall, we stopped at another office. "Our nurse's office."

"You have a nurse on staff?" Arthur asked.

I didn't want to tell him that I'd hired Hugo to look after Breakthrough patients, so I faked a smile. "In case of emergencies."

I stuck my head into Hugo's office and said hello. When Hugo turned from his desk and smiled, I introduced him to Arthur.

"Please let us know if there's anything you need during your stay," Hugo said.

We continued down the hallway, reaching my office at the end. "This is my consultation room."

Arthur admired my collection of Carl Jung's works on the bookshelf and smiled as he noticed a portrait of Melanie Klein, a pioneering psycho-analyst, on the wall.

He opened his arms with pride. "The place is incredible, truly." He checked the time on his phone. "So, listen, Naomi and I are planning a swim across Walden Pond. You said there was something you wanted to show me?"

I nodded and walked over to the door leading to the basement. Open-ing the door, I led him and Kendall down the stairs. When we reached the bottom of the stairs, I turned to Arthur and said, "I just want you to keep an open mind."

He glanced at me sideways. "That sounds a little ominous."

As we walked down the hall, Arthur paused at the first room. Inside, the bed was occupied by Max. His face was sweaty, and a bowl of urine sat next to the bed.

Standing in the doorway, Arthur asked, "What is this?"

I ushered him into the room. "You know how fed up I am with reductionist medicine, and how I've embraced psychosomatic and integrative ways of thinking—pretty much the path you followed your whole career." I glanced down at Max. "Well, through our new program, we're pushing the boundaries of psychiatry."

Arthur glanced at Max, then studied me skeptically. "What's wrong with this man? You're saying there are more like him?"

"We've graduated five patients from Project Breakthrough in which we induce brief periods of illness to stimulate a post-traumatic growth. Max is part of our second wave."

Arthur frowned. "You're joking, right?"

Standing in the doorway, Kendall shook her head. "All our patients consented to undergo a voluntary sickness to improve their lives."

Arthur turned to stare at me as if I were a stranger. "I don't even know where to begin. Did you forget your oath, Calvin: 'First do no harm'?"

I raised my hands placatingly. "Believe me, I was just as skeptical as you when we first started talking about the program. But it works, Art. It *really* works."

My mentor shook his head, clearly unconvinced.

"I proved the concept as the program's first patient," Kendall added. "I experienced a breakthrough in my writing after I recovered."

He ignored Kendall's argument and glared at me. "A doctor's role is to *heal* people, not make them sick."

Kendall stepped closer. "These people finally have time to pause their busy lives, look inward, and figure some things out. How many people get the chance to do that?"

Arthur wasn't buying it. "People's personalities don't just change after some weeks-long illness you manufacture in a basement," he said. "Anyone who's gone through therapy knows that psychological change happens slowly. Years can go by without much change." He pointed at me. "You of all people should know that."

"But what if we've underestimated the normal speed of psychological change, Arthur?" I asked, gesturing between myself and Kendall. "Both of us had something profound happen to us. I experienced personal growth after psychosomatic illness; Kendall had a creative breakthrough following her sickness. And they happened in weeks, not years."

"This is beyond unethical, maybe even illegal." Arthur shook his head disapprovingly.

It saddened me to see my mentor react to Project Breakthrough so negatively. But how could I blame him? He was giving voice to the same concerns I'd had—and still had, to some degree. I rubbed my temples, feeling a migraine take hold.

Seeing I was in pain, Kendall tried to take control of the situation, perhaps protect me. "This is a revolution in psychiatry, sir. Instead of resisting, why don't you join us, and we can do something new and exciting together."

Arthur laughed humorlessly. A man of science, I didn't expect him to be convinced by Kendall's rhetoric. In truth, I wasn't always either.

"Whatever's going on here," Arthur said, his voice sharp with disappointment, "I want nothing to do with it. You're playing with fire, and someone's going to get hurt."

Marching toward the door, he paused before stepping out of the room. Glancing at me, he pointed at Kendall. "She's a bad influence on you, Calvin."

Kendall waved at him mockingly. "Always nice seeing you, Dr. *Bratt.*"

Shaking his head, Arthur stormed out of the room and up the stairs. Kendall and I stood there, saying nothing, until the slam of the front door echoed through the building.

Was Arthur right? Had I let Kendall push me too far? Was something bad coming? I didn't know what to say, and my head hurt so badly, I could barely think straight. "I need to go lie down."

"Do you want something to eat first?" Kendall asked.

"No, thank you. I'm not hungry." I caught my reflection in the mirror and noticed a cold sore blooming on my lower lip. "I just need to rest."

"I don't like seeing you so stressed, Cal." She lowered her voice to a whisper. "I'd hate for what happened to you on your cross-country trip to happen again."

It was sweet of Kendall to worry, but I'd learned, and grown, from that experience. "That won't happen again."

Chapter Twenty-One

That night, I lay in bed, staring at the cracks in the ceiling, wide awake. It wasn't so much the splitting headache that kept me up as Arthur's reaction to Project Breakthrough. I admired him as a physician, as a mentor, as a man, and his reaction to our program devastated me. He thought I'd ignored my own conscience and violated my oath as a physician. Did he really think Kendall and I were breaking the law?

I thought about what Kendall had said, too—that we weren't doing anything wrong and that we'd started a revolution in psychiatry. As a physician, I was trained to keep a level head about experimental programs, especially when they involved patients. As such, I'd always tried to balance my enthusiasm for the project's potential with the real possibility that we could mess up at any time.

Except for that one small crack in her conviction after Gavin's review, Kendall had begun talking like a zealot, and her true belief concerned me. I knew we had to talk about making changes to the program, but my head felt like it was being crushed and I couldn't think straight. Just thinking about hitting pause on Project Breakthrough calmed me, and somehow, I drifted off.

When morning came, I went to the bathroom and washed my face. I'd slept at least six hours, which normally would've been enough for me to feel rested, but my head still throbbed and I couldn't shake the exhaustion and brain fog that made thinking difficult. Intellectually, I knew these symptoms were stress related, not indications of some underlying disease, but I couldn't help but wonder if something was starting to go wrong with my body. Was it turning on me again?

More questions churned in my mind: What if the migraines grew more intense, more frequent? What if the fatigue got so bad, I couldn't work? What if I experienced more symptoms? What if what happened during my trip was happening again? What if it was *worse* this time around?

I managed to take a shower and went downstairs. Normally, I would've made eggs or a smoothie for breakfast, but I had no appetite. Knowing my body needed fuel, I looked for something small to eat.

I was peeling a banana when Kendall burst into the kitchen, with a horrified look on her face. "Calvin! Oh, thank God."

My back straightened, and I stopped peeling. "What is it?"

"You need to come downstairs right now!"

She ran out of the kitchen. I dropped the banana and followed. "Kendall, what's going on?"

Opening the basement door, she called back over her shoulder, "Max is unconscious, isn't responding."

We rushed into Max's room, where Hugo was holding one of Max's eyelids open and shining a light into his eye.

"Talk to me, Hugo," I said, worried. "What's going on?"

Max's movements were slow, labored.

"Not sure, but vitals don't look good," Hugo shot back.

Kendall was pacing alongside the bed, chewing a fingertip nervously.

I turned to her. "Were you here when this happened?"

She ran a hand through her hair. "I was just asking him what he wanted for breakfast when he said he felt nauseous, and his legs were tingly and numb. Then he vomited and started garbling his words. The last thing he said before he passed out was . . ."

"What?" I demanded.

"*Walden.*"

"Has he ever used the safe word before?"

"First time I've heard *any* patient use it."

I anxiously rubbed my beard, worrying out loud about what might be happening to Max. "Severe bradycardia . . . could be cardiogenic shock."

Kendall threw up her hands. "What the hell does that mean?"

"His heart can't pump enough blood to meet the body's needs."

Hugo pressed two fingers to Max's neck. "Barely feel a pulse now."

"Whatever it is, we're not equipped to offer the medical attention he needs." I pulled out my phone and dialed 911. "I'm calling an ambulance."

I stared at the floor blankly once the call was done.

Kendall gripped my shoulder and spoke in a measured tone. "Stay calm, Calvin. Every patient signed an agreement that protects us from legal action."

I stared at her disbelievingly. "A patient might die under our care, and you're worried about legal trouble?"

She didn't flinch. "Someone has to look out for that kind of stuff."

I studied her face, feeling a quiet distance from the girlfriend I knew.

Ten minutes later, paramedics arrived and loaded Max onto a stretcher. They'd cut away his oversized shirt and sweatpants, and his immense frame strained the metal. They said he'd suffered from cardiogenic shock, likely caused by early heart failure.

In the driveway, I watched as the stretcher was loaded into the ambulance. A few feet away, Kendall paced as she talked on the phone with our lawyer, trying to get ahead of any potential liability issues.

Hugo approached me sheepishly. "I'm sorry, Dr. Bloom," he said. "I think it was a mistake for me to come here. I should probably go back to what I was doing before."

I tried to respond, but for some reason, I couldn't find the words. I wanted to tell him this incident wasn't his fault, but a mental slowness stopped me from speaking.

Hugo squinted at me. "Dr. Bloom? Are you alright?"

I rubbed my forehead and closed my eyes, trying to concentrate. Somehow, I managed to speak. "I'm . . . I'm fine."

Kendall got off the phone and walked toward us. When she reached us, she frowned at me and put a hand on my forehead.

"My goodness, you're running a fever. Let's get you to bed. I'll go to the hospital after and sort this mess out."

I nodded solemnly.

Hugo raised a finger. "Um, Kendall?"

She spun to face him. "What is it, Hugo?"

He bit his lip and glanced at the ambulance. "I think I need to leave. This is all too much for me."

She glared at him. "You're abandoning us?" She looked over her shoulder at the center, then looked at Hugo worriedly. "You're abandoning your patients?"

He scratched the back of his head, looking conflicted.

"Hugo?" I asked.

The nurse exhaled and then muttered, "Fine, I'll stay for this last batch of patients, but then I'm out. I'd like to keep my license, you know?"

"Very well," Kendall said.

I didn't want to see Hugo go, but I understood his decision, perhaps even envied it. After this job, he could go anywhere. The Bloom Center was my life, my career, and it had completely consumed me. Actually, it was Project Breakthrough that had taken over, and it could end up destroying everything.

We all parted and once inside, I froze at the stairs. I'd climbed them a hundred times before, but now they felt like a gauntlet. Kendall saw me and rushed over to help. As we ascended, she wrapped an arm around me to keep me from falling over.

I collapsed into bed as soon as we reached it and groaned as the pain of another migraine stabbed my brain. She helped me out of my clothes and pulled the covers over me, expressing how glad she was that I'd made it to bed safely. It was midmorning, yet I was bone-tired and felt like I could sleep for days.

She kissed me on the forehead. "You rest, dear. I'll take care of every-thing."

I closed my eyes. "Thank you." She turned to leave, but there was something I needed to say. "Kendall?"

She spun around. "Yes, dear?"

"What if we've gone too far?"

She shook her head. "How do you mean?"

"With Project Breakthrough."

She didn't respond, just stared at me across the dimly lit room.

"Someone almost died today," I said quietly.

I studied Kendall's face, feeling like I could peer straight into her soul. Then I saw it: a flash, barely a second, a flicker of doubt—just like after Gavin's review—like maybe we'd screwed up, like maybe she'd lost her way. But just as fast as it came, it vanished, and the program's true believer was back.

She sat on the edge of the bed. "A hiccup was bound to happen at some point, Cal. We're reimagining the path to healing; of course there will be missteps, even a few accidents. You know what they say: you have to break a few eggs to make an omelet."

How could she so glibly minimize what had happened? Everything I'd worked so hard for was now at risk. I'd reached a turning point, and when patients were at risk, the decision was easy.

"This needs to stop, Kendall."

"We hit a bump in the road," she said, reassuringly. "We just have to be more careful going forward."

"It's gone far enough!"

Her expression cooled. "On the contrary, I think we need to go *further.*"

The migraine tightened its grip on my head. "What are you talking about?"

"I've been researching drugs we could use to make patients even sicker."

Searching her face, I saw that she was dead serious. "A patient of ours is probably in the ICU right now, and might die, and you want to make people *sicker?*"

"Think about it, Cal. The greater the suffering, the *bigger* the breakthrough. Makes sense, right? Isn't that what this program is all about?"

That logic was warped. But I didn't have the energy to explain how wrong she was, no matter how concerned her radical thinking made me.

"How would you know when to stop?" I managed to ask. "How sick is too sick?"

She exhaled heavily. "So, it's finally come to this."

"Come to what?"

"I always knew you wouldn't have the backbone to realize our program's true potential. Perhaps you've forgotten? If I hadn't made myself sick, there wouldn't even *be* a Project Breakthrough. So, it looks like I'll have to take the next step without you."

"What are you talking about? What are you planning?"

"Why tell you, when I can show you."

Chapter Twenty-Two

When I woke, I felt like I hadn't slept at all. But I needed to get out of bed and try to dissuade Kendall from carrying out her plans. Before moving, I tried to recall what I'd said the night before, but I had trouble bringing forth the memory. All I could remember was thinking she was wrong, maybe dangerous, possibly out of her mind.

As I swung my legs off the side of the bed, my stomach turned. Rushing into the bathroom, I emptied the contents of my stomach into the toilet. Once I'd stopped retching, I slumped to the side of the toilet and laid my spinning head on the cold linoleum floor.

Just then, I heard my bedroom door open.

"Cal? Where are you?" Walking into the bathroom, Kendall bent over me and rubbed my leg. "Oh, bub, you look awful." She tugged at my shirt, and I groaned. "C'mon, let's get you back into bed."

As she helped me off the floor, the world spun once again. Dropping back to my knees in front of the toilet, I vomited again as Kendall rubbed the back of my head.

When it finally let up, I wiped my mouth with my shirt. "What's wrong with me? I've never felt this bad."

She pulled me to my feet, wrapping my arm over her shoulder, and we inched our way out of the bathroom. "You know how you can get when you're under a lot of pressure."

Were these symptoms the result of stress? Maybe she was right. I just needed to lie down and get my thoughts straight. But my head felt heavy and unfocused.

"Almost there," Kendall said, keeping me upright as we approached the bed. The moment we were close enough, I crashed into bed, and she propped my head up with a pillow.

"What's going to happen if I can't run the center?" I asked worriedly. "What about my patients?"

"I'll call your patients and tell them you're not feeling well and that you'll be back at it in a day or two."

"And Project Breakthrough?"

"I know you have reservations. We'll talk about them when you're feeling better, all right?"

I didn't have the energy to debate, and another wave of nausea welled up inside me. "Can you get me a bucket, please? I can't make it to—.""

Kendall grabbed a bucket, and I heaved into it as she rubbed my head. Once she'd wiped my mouth with a towel, I laid my head back on the pillow.

"I need you to know something," I said.

"What is it, Cal?"

"If my symptoms get worse—if I become like I was in on my cross-country trip—I want you to know that you don't have to stick around and take care of me. I've seen people care for chronically ill loved ones, and I don't want that for you."

Kendall's face softened. "You took care of me when I was sick. Why wouldn't I do the same for you? No matter how bad things get, I'll always be there for you."

"But what if there's something seriously wrong with me and things get really bad?"

Until that moment, I hadn't really considered the possibility that I might not recover or that whatever was happening to me might be life-threatening.

Kendall leaned in close and rubbed my face. "I'd rather have a short life with you than a long life with someone else."

Even though Kendall seemed to have become a different person from the woman I'd known before we started Project Breakthrough, it felt so good to hear those words. It felt good to be cared for, loved. Despite everything that had happened, and everything Kendall had been saying recently, I realized that I still loved her—and I told her that.

She smiled warmly. "I love you too."

I closed my eyes, and she rubbed my head until I felt asleep.

Chapter Twenty-Three

Days passed, and autumn came to New England. Through my window, I watched the forest explode with reds, yellows, and oranges. The temperatures dipped into the fifties, and I spent my days in bed, wrapped in blankets, longing for a time when my body didn't feel like it was grinding to a halt.

With my permission, Kendall had informed my patients I was taking an extended sick leave, and she and Hugo continued caring for the Breakthrough patients.

Initially, I thought bed rest would be the best therapy for whatever ailed me, but my symptoms only got worse after I took to bed. Whenever Kendall or Hugo asked me where it hurt, I'd simply say everywhere. No system was spared. Head, stomach, back—everything was in pain.

No matter how long I slept, I always felt exhausted. Unpredictable spells of nausea, debilitating headaches, and brain fog became constant companions. My lymph nodes were swollen and tender, and my appetite was practically nonexistent. My throat felt hot from acid reflux, and there was a near-constant sharp pain in my stomach.

One day, my ears started ringing and never stopped. I thought the high-pitched sound would eventually drive me crazy, especially in the quiet of the night, but I learned to avoid focusing on it. Hugo had the good idea of turning on a fan before going to sleep to drown out the noise in my head.

Because of my neurological symptoms, it was hard to feel human. I had short-term memory problems and issues with executive function, like difficulty planning and organizing. Sometimes, I'd have trouble remembering words, like the time I couldn't remember the word *fork* when Kendall brought me dinner. Spatial disorientation made it feel unsafe to leave bed, so I ate every meal there.

Once, I managed to get myself out of bed because I wanted to admire the foliage outside my window, but by the time I reached the middle of the room, I'd forgotten where I was and why I'd gotten up. I paid a high price for the adventure too. The effort caused severe fatigue that left me unable to move my body for a day.

I also developed physical symptoms that felt like arthritis. My knees swelled and ached, followed by my fingers, elbows, shoulders, neck, and spine. I was taking the maximum amount of painkillers I could in a day. Hugo had tried glucosamine tablets, heat treatments, and even various topical remedies without success. Eventually, the joint symptoms limited my mobility so much that I could barely leave my bed, an activity I soon lost interest in anyway.

One day, as I lay staring at the ceiling, my head pounding from a migraine, I realized that this wasn't my cross-country trip all over again—it was worse. My body had gone completely haywire, betraying me. Like our Breakthrough patients, I was now bedridden. As Kendall put it in her essay, I was living in the kingdom of the ill.

Whenever Kendall had a spare moment in her daily schedule, she'd visit my room. Sometimes, she'd sit next to my bed and tell me about the day-to-day happenings of the center and how my patients had been calling to say they wished I'd getter better soon. Other times, she'd read to me, preferring the work of Virginia Woolf, who wrote about her own illness and considered it a portal to self-understanding.

One day, Kendall chose Woolf's essay "On Being Ill" to read to me.

Considering how common illness is, how tremendous the spiritual change that it brings . . . it becomes strange indeed that illness has not taken its place with love and battle and jealousy among the prime themes of literature.

I told her that Woolf's words had resonated with me. "Now I know what our patients feel when they're really sick."

She lowered the book. "It's good for a doctor to experience what their patients do. It gives them a window into disease, builds empathy, makes them a better provider."

I explained it wasn't just the symptoms that made being sick such a horrible experience. It was the boredom. Being confined to my bed, unable to go anywhere or do much of anything, time seemed to stand still. In search of stimulation, my mind turned inward. The deep introspection had yielded some interesting insights about myself and life, but they were fleeting. I couldn't remember most of them.

Some of what I did remember had to do with sickness, and how it fit into Project Breakthrough. For a long time, Kendall and I had been working from the same assumption: that suffering was clarifying, that sickness automatically delivered insight—that it stripped things down, made life sharper. But lying in bed, I was realizing that wasn't necessarily true. My thoughts felt messier than ever. Each day seemed worse, not better. When I told Kendall this, she surprised me by partially agreeing.

"Sometimes the insights don't come while you're ill. They come after," she explained. "If they don't show up, you just have to go looking for them."

She said she had something for me, left the room, and returned with a spiral-bound notebook. "Why don't you write down your thoughts? It could help you make sense of what's happening."

I took the notebook and rubbed my thumb along the cover. "My head's kind of a mess," I said. "Writing might be hard, but I'll try. Any advice?"

She looked at the Woolf's book on the bedside table. "Write about yourself, but find what's universal in it. And try to tell a story."

"Maybe that's why some readers saw my piece about psychosomatic illness as navel-gazing," I said. "Even a little narcissistic."

Nodding, Kendall explained how she'd written the essay that had resonated with so many people. "I tried to enlarge my introspections beyond my own experiences, from the personal to the general, from the particular to the universal."

"That's good advice, thank you." I paused. "I wish I could talk to Art about all of this. I know he's mad, but would you mind calling him to see if he'll visit?"

"Oh, he's probably too busy," Kendall replied quickly. "Plus, I don't think you're really well enough for visitors, bub."

"Please, Kendall."

She looked conflicted, but said she'd give him a call.

Thankfully, when she came back that afternoon, she told me she'd managed to convince Arthur to visit by telling him that I was in poor health.

Given how we'd left things, I wasn't sure how the visit would go.

Chapter Twenty-Four

When Arthur arrived a day later, he didn't look mad. In fact, he appeared rather joyful as he entered my room carrying a full canvas bag.

I gave him a quick once-over, admiring the multicolored parrots on his shirt.

"I bet Naomi loves that one," I said with a grin.

"She tried to throw it away! Can you believe that?"

I shook my head in jest. "Some people have no taste."

Arthur dropped the bag on the bed next to me. "I come bearing gifts."

I propped my back up against the headboard. "What do you have there?"

"Kendall said you weren't feeling well, so I brought you some reading material."

"That's very kind of you, Art."

"I remember you saying you liked reading fiction written by doctors but that you hadn't read a lot of nonfiction by them. I brought a few of my favorites."

Arthur started pulling books from his bag. "Paul Kalanithi's memoir, Atul Gawande's book on mortality, and, of course, a few classics by Oliver Sacks."

One by one, I stacked the books on my nightstand, only pausing when he placed the final book in my hands. It was *his* new book: *Putting the We in Medicine.*

"Congratulations! I can't wait to read it." Placing it at the top of the stack, I looked over my new to-be-read pile. "Thank you for bringing me these. I'm hoping to do some of my own writing, so these should offer some good inspiration."

Arthur sat on the edge of my bed and patted my leg. "So, listen. You know how I feel about this program of yours, but I won't try to convince you to stop. Believe it or not, I might even be coming around to what you're trying to do."

I raised my eyebrows. "Yeah?"

He looked out my window, toward the forest, bright with fall colors. "Have you ever heard of the evolutionary theory punctuated equilibrium?"

I shook my head.

"It argues that some evolutionary changes don't occur gradually, but rather in intense, rapid spurts triggered by dramatic environmental pressures."

I urged him to offer an example.

"Think about a species of birds living comfortably on an island," he said. "For thousands of years, nothing much changes. Then a drought hits and most of the food disappears. Within just a few generations, only the birds with slightly longer, stronger beaks survive. Suddenly, the species looks different. That rapid shift, followed by another long stretch of stability—that's punctuated equilibrium."

I got it immediately. "You think that's how Project Breakthrough works?"

"For years, the body can seem stable," he said, nodding. "You live inside it without thinking much about how it works. Then illness strikes. Everything changes at once—how you move, how you think, how time feels. The nervous system scrambles, rewiring itself just to get through the crisis."

"And you're okay with the ethics of the program?"

"It goes against almost everything I know as a doctor, but forcing someone to become sick might act like intense environmental pressure, which could trigger a powerful change in personality."

"You'll probably be interested to know that our program didn't start working until I discovered a missing ingredient."

"What's that?"

"Our patients weren't responding until we started talking with them more often, listening and laughing with them, and letting them hang out and play together outside of their rooms. That's when they started having breakthroughs."

Arthur let out a low "mm," as if urging me to keep going.

"Even though they're sick, exhausted, cut off from family and friends, and stuck in bed for long stretches, I think our patients are having some of the best times of their lives." I laughed. "Pretty sure two of our patients even fell in love."

He smiled, and placed a hand on my shoulder. "I'm sorry for not believing in you at first, Calvin. You might be doing something special here."

Something in my chest relaxed. It felt good to hear my mentor say those words, for him to finally see the value in what we were doing, even as I found myself questioning it more and more.

Arthur moved from my bed to the chair beside it. "Now, I'd like to talk about your health, if you're feeling up to it."

I realized I was seeing the bedside manner he'd described in his memoir.

"What do you think is going on?" he asked.

I shook my head. "It's hard to say exactly, given how many systems are being affected. I'm having neurological, gastrointestinal, cardiovascular, and orthopedic symptoms. I thought about autoimmune conditions, like multiple sclerosis or rheumatoid arthritis, but I honestly don't know."

"Autoimmune is . . . possible," Arthur agreed slowly. "And I could help you arrange blood work, if you want to seek a diagnosis."

"But?"

His gaze was compassionate as it met mine. "Have you considered that what's happening now might be the same thing that happened to during your road trip?"

"That was my first thought," I said, nodding solemnly. "But this feels worse than what happened to me a few years ago."

"The increased severity could just mean you're more stressed than you were before or that your body is less able to tolerate the stress and the symptoms its causing."

I gnawed on my lip. Was Arthur right? The symptoms were similar to the ones I had during my trip; it was only the severity of my current condition that made me look beyond what I'd already experienced.

After a long silence, I nodded. "What do you recommend I do?"

"What you're experiencing reminds me of Naomi and how over-whelming the demands of her work life became when we first met."

"I enjoy your company, Art, but I'm not marrying you too."

Arthur laughed. "I just think you should keep taking it easy. Read, relax, maybe write. Do all the things that got you out of the hole you were in after you got sick."

I recalled my drive back to Boston, haunting bookstores and discovering books that helped me get better. "Alright, Doc," I said. "I'll do as you say."

Walking across the room, Arthur cracked open the window. "And let in this fresh New England air from time to time. Nature's medicine."

"It's good to know this is probably my body speaking again," I said. "A reminder that stress, anxiety, and depression can show up as almost anything."

Arthur slapped me on the thigh. "You'll be on the road to recovery in no time! And when the time comes, it might also be worth doing some therapy of your own to identify the thoughts that might've played a role in the development of your symptoms."

I thought I already knew what stressors had led to my current state, but I didn't dare tell Arthur my worries about Kendall right now. Instead, I took a deep breath and released it slowly. "Thanks for coming by, Art. I really appreciate it."

"Listen, I want to see you get better. You're far too talented a shrink—and too nice a guy—to be stuck in this bed all day like this."

I smiled, my eyes softening with gratitude.

Arthur stood and paused thoughtfully. "You know, it may have taken a while for me to wrap my head around this program of yours, but it does ring true with something I've always told patients who are going through a sickness."

"What's that?"

"Never waste an illness," he said. "You could be in this bed for a while. If you can, try to do something useful with the time."

Chapter Twenty-Five

Inspired by Arthur's visit and Kendall's insistence that I write about what was happening, I decided to get some words down after he left. I didn't feel strong enough to sit at the desk, but I'd always found writing in bed comfortable anyway. Sitting with my back against the headboard, I positioned my notebook on my knees. As I held my pen over a blank page, Arthur's words rang in my ears. "Never waste an illness."

I made a decision to write about the last few years of my life. I began with my fateful choice to postpone my medical career and, instead, go on a long-distance drive to think and write. I wrote without a plan or an outline, exploring what I thought had gone wrong on my trip across the country and why my illness had developed.

As the words spilled out, new insights revealed themselves. I realized I could've stayed in medicine and tried to land a residency in California before I left. Planning my trip better would've made me less stressed, too. I could've rented a place out there before I left instead of waiting to make the decision about where to live when I arrived.

I was in the middle of developing a thought when I heard footsteps on the staircase. I turned to the door, eager to tell Kendall about my conversation with Arthur and plan to write a story, maybe even a book.

The figure who appeared in the doorway, however, was not her.

"Hugo, what are you—"

"Shh!" Hugo held a finger to his lips. Glancing over his shoulder, he ducked into the room.

"What's wrong?"

Hugo darted across the room and knelt beside me. "Dr. Bloom, we don't have much time to talk; I need to tell you something."

I tried to sit up taller and groaned. "Whatever it is, you can tell me."

Hugo's eyes were wide, fearful. "Your symptoms, your illness—I don't think they're happening naturally."

"Well, in a way you're right," I said. "At the very least, the cause isn't physical. I'm sure you know Arthur was just here. He believes, and I agree, that this a resurgence of what happened to me a few years ago."

"That's the thing! Kendall told me what was going on with you, and I don't think this is the same as what you experienced before."

I shook my head. "No, Art and I agreed this is a functional neurological disorder, when psychological distress converts into physical symptoms—"

"I know what psychosomatic illness is, Dr. Bloom." Hugo leaned in close and whispered, "What if that's what Kendall *wants* you to think it is?"

I frowned, confused. "What does she have to do with this?"

He lowered his head. "I overheard Kendall on the phone when she called Dr. Pratt to ask him to visit and again this morning when she greeted him. Both times, she mentioned what happened to you on your cross-country trip."

"So?" I shook my head. "She's been worried for a while now that I'd have a resurgence. Just because she was right—"

"But she wasn't! She's been planting the idea in yours and Dr. Pratt's heads to hide what she's *really* up to."

I eyed Hugo, bewildered. "And what's that?"

"Her sick little experiment."

"Experiment? On what?"

"On our patients! On *you*, Dr. Bloom. For Project Breakthrough."

"You're not making any sense, Hugo."

I grabbed my notebook, intending to get back to writing.

"Listen, a patient in the second batch of Breakthrough patients has the exact same symptoms you're having. I was curious, so I went through our medical notes." He glanced at the door warily. "The patient's on a chemotherapy drug."

I shook my head. "That can't be. You come to me every time you need a prescription, and I've never approved a drug that strong."

Pulling out his phone, Hugo showed me a picture of a prescription for a chemotherapy medicine. "That's your signature, right?"

It was. "How can that be?"

"I don't know. Maybe Kendall got you to sign it when you were really out of it, or maybe she forged the signature. She seems capable of anything, honestly."

I couldn't believe what I was hearing. "That's against the law. If anyone found out, I could lose my medical license." I thought for a moment. "Wait, what happened to the patient who was put on chemo?"

"That patient was Max."

"Oh my God."

"He spent a week in the ICU, but he's going to live," Hugo said. "I think Kendall covered her tracks so the doctors wouldn't suspect foul play."

I had so many thoughts, so many worries. But first, I needed to address the most disturbing possibility. "Are you saying Kendall is poisoning patients . . . poisoning *me*?"

Hugo bit his lip, then nodded.

Why would she do this? Just as I had the thought, I remembered our last conversation. "She thinks if patients suffer more, they'll have bigger breakthroughs. That's why she chose a chemotherapy agent. It'll devastate the body and mind."

"I think she wants to give chemo to all of our patients, Dr. Bloom."

I was horrified. There was no way to tell how patients would react to the chemo. No way to predict the side effects. This was bad, very bad.

"Someone could die on this drug," I said. "I could die!"

"We should call the police."

I grabbed Hugo's arm. "We need proof first. Can you get me those medical charts?"

Hugo nodded and opened his phone again. He scrolled through his image gallery before turning the phone around to show me the drug he'd administered circled in red.

"Send those to me," I told him.

He typed on his phone. "Done."

Chapter Twenty-Six

Maybe thirty minutes later, Kendall strolled into my room. I was sitting up in bed, writing, skipping ahead in my story and trying to recreate the conversation I'd just had with Hugo for a future scene.

Looking chipper, Kendall carried in a tray holding a cup of coffee and a muffin, which she set on the nightstand beside me. "How's my little trooper feeling?"

I faked a smile. I was too sick, too disturbed by the situation, and too scared about my health to respond with levity. In truth, I'd never felt worse. It felt like someone had hit me in the face with a shovel. All I could think about was that I was being poisoned by the woman standing in front of me, this woman who I thought I knew. Thought I loved.

"I have a special surprise for you," she said.

I raised my eyebrows. "Oh, yeah?"

"If you're feeling up to it, of course."

The only thing I felt "up to" was confronting my girlfriend about secretly giving me a dangerous drug to keep me in bed so she could covertly expand our program into something criminal, maybe sadistic.

For some reason, though, I couldn't spit the words out. Kendall tended to steamroll me, and, increasingly, it felt harder to resist her. Clearly, she wanted to show me something, and as usual, I felt like I had to see it through before I spoke my truth.

I exhaled sharply. "Let's see what you've got."

Smiling, she walked to the doorway and stuck her head around the corner. "All right, guys. Come on in!"

To my astonishment, the room began to fill with faces I couldn't forget even if I tried: the first graduates from Project Breakthrough. One by one, Chase, Annette, Abby, and Jordan—everyone except Gavin—stood quietly at the foot of my bed. Their smiles were small, strange, almost hesitant, like they were trying to be comforting in a way I couldn't quite grasp. *What the hell is going on here?*

Kendall strode around the group with her hands clasped behind her back. "Take a good look, Cal. Here are your success stories. The brave souls who took great risks to go through our program and, as intended, achieved the breakthroughs they desired."

I cleared my throat, feeling a bit overwhelmed. "It's nice to see you all again."

"I invited the gang back so you could hear how they've been doing since graduating . . . how they've changed for the better."

Kendall nodded at Chase, who stepped forward. "Hi, Dr. Bloom, good to see you again. I quit my marketing job and applied to PhD programs in anthropology." He smiled widely, his blue eyes like glacial ice. "I got into the program of my dreams. I have this whole life waiting for me now, and I can't wait to start it."

"That's wonderful, Chase," I replied. "I'm very happy for you."

Kendall nodded at Annette, who shuffled toward my bed and stood shoulder-to-shoulder with Chase. "When I got home, I filed for divorce." She laughed self-consciously. "My time here gave me the clarity I needed to leave the bastard. And guess what?" She lifted her left hand to show off a diamond-studded engagement ring, then leaned into Chase and wrapped her arms around him.

"You guys?" I said. "That's great!"

Stepping forward, Jordan rolled his eyes. "Like we didn't all see *that* coming."

Annette turned and kicked Jordan in the thigh.

Kendall was clapping as if she were at the circus. "Go, Jordan!"

Jordan rubbed his leg, pretending Annette's kick had been painful. "Well, I'm still teaching high school, but I bought a food truck and drive it around my local beach on weekends. Everyone loves it. I love it! It's the most fun I've had in years."

"We'll have to come by and try your food someday," I replied.

Abby laughed and tilted her head toward Jordan. "Maybe the Bloom Center could use Jordan's food to make patients sick?"

Jordan pinched the bridge of his nose. "I hate you. So much."

Abby, who now seemed to embrace her curves with confidence, said her Breakthrough experience had inspired her to enroll in a documentary filmmaking program. Another success story.

I genuinely enjoyed hearing how our program had improved our patients' lives, but I couldn't help but wonder if Kendall had engineered this stunt just to manipulate me. When everyone had finished, she opened her arms to encompass the group.

"See this, Cal? See what you did? What *we* did? You were spinning your wheels at your former clinic, but here at the Bloom Center, through Project Breakthrough, you're actually helping people become better versions of themselves."

I mustered the strength to sit up higher and address the group. "Thank you all for sharing your stories. My dream has always been to help people uncover the conflicts hidden deep within them and spark the transformation they've been longing for. Hearing your stories has assured me that I've done what I set out to do."

Even as I spoke, I wondered what Project Breakthrough had cost us. Max had nearly died in the ICU, and now Kendall was sickening me and other patients.

I stared at her, not hiding my contempt. "And I suppose my sickness is leading to some great breakthrough, too?"

Recognizing I was upset, Kendall turned to our former patients. "Thank you all again for coming to visit. Dr. Bloom hasn't been feeling well, so let's give him some space now. Hugo will see you out."

One by one, Chase, Annette, Abby and Jordon thanked me again and filed out of the room to meet Hugo in the hallway. Kendall shut the door behind the last one and approached the foot of my bed.

"I know you're struggling, hun, but I do think your sickness is leading to something great." She circled the bed, coming closer. "I need you to accept this. I promise: an awakening is coming."

I laughed incredulously. "My body is failing me, Kendall."

She shook her head. "I think you're going to be Breakthrough's greatest success."

Looking into her eyes, I couldn't understand how she'd become the person in front of me. In that moment, I knew she was lost. I needed to confront her with the truth.

Grabbing my phone off the nightstand, I pulled up the photo of medical notes Hugo had sent me. I turned the phone around for her to see.

She took the phone out of my hand and studied the screen. Her face scrunched into a scowl. "I knew Hugo would betray me."

"How could you do this to me?"

She slipped my phone into her pocket. "I'm doing what you can't do yourself. What you need me to do *for you*."

"Why would I want to *poison* myself?"

Kendall knew she'd been caught, but she looked defiant.

"You must see the logic in it, Calvin? You're Project Breakthrough's perfect patient. Think of the self-knowledge you obtained after your health scare years ago. Your illness humbled you, gave you empathy for your patients. I'm giving you the chance to be sicker than you've ever been. Imagine the benefits that could come from this level of suffering. Not just for you, but for your future patients."

Somehow, Kendall couldn't see how warped her thinking and behavior really were. She'd rationalized her actions, and there was no getting through to her.

"What happened to you, Kendall?"

She ignored the question. "Please don't worry, bub. I know the chemo is causing you a lot of pain, but I'm taking care of you, just like you took care of me."

I reached out my hand. "I'd like my phone back, please."

"You don't need any distractions right now." She covered my leg with a blanket and patted it gently. "You need to focus on your healing."

Tears welled up in my eyes, but she didn't seem to notice. For days, I'd been stuck in a prison of my own suffering, and now I was being held captive by the woman I loved.

She needed to be stopped, but how? How could I get the truth out? How could I possibly outmaneuver her? Every day I felt weaker, and I was starting to wonder if I'd ever get out of bed again.

Chapter Twenty-Seven

Later that evening, my health took a turn for the worse. My body aching all over, I contorted into a fetal position in bed. The dizziness and nausea was worse than ever. Every fifteen minutes or so, I'd lean over the edge of my bed to vomit into a bucket.

I was just pulling back from one such episode when I glanced at my pillow and froze, horrified. A new symptom: the pillow was covered in clumps of hair.

An unexpected rage welled up inside me. Snatching my pillow, I shook it as hard as I could and watched the thin gray hairs rain down on the floor. Then I threw the pillow onto the bed, smashed my face into it, and screamed.

I heard the door crack open. "Who's there?" I demanded.

"Dr. Bloom?" a voice whispered.

"Hugo, that you?"

The nurse slunk into the room. "Can I come in?"

I groaned.

As Hugo approached, I saw he was holding something in his hand, but I couldn't make out what it was. He dropped into the chair beside my bed and scooted it closer.

"I brought something for you, to help you get around." He raised his hand high enough for me to recognize a walking cane.

It was a sweet gesture. "Thanks, buddy. But I think my walking days are over."

Glancing at the nightstand, he grabbed the bottle of hand lotion that sat there. He squirted some lotion into his palm. "Give me your hand."

"Why?"

"I do this with all the Breakthrough patients. It helps, trust me."

I held out my right hand, trusting that Hugo had my best interests in mind. Taking my hand in both of his, he slowly rubbed the lotion into my palm. "That feel okay?"

It was so relaxing. "Very soothing, yes."

He pressed his thumb into my palm and rubbed in a circular motion. "Did you talk to Kendall?"

I nodded. "She thinks poisoning me is going to lead to some big breakthrough."

"I was afraid of that." Hugo kept rubbing gently. "Try not to think about any of that right now. Just focus on this sensation."

I breathed deeply and focused on the warm feeling. After a few minutes, Hugo switched to my other hand. As he rubbed, he squinted at the nightstand beside him and lifted his chin to indicate my notebook. "I noticed you were writing in this when I visited last time."

"Kendall and Arthur encouraged me to write while I'm sick."

Hugo pushed his hand against my open palm, stretching my fingers. "You've been able to write in your state?"

"Even if I'm really suffering, I've been able to push myself to record what's been happening. It's helping me make sense of things."

"Have you written about . . . her?"

"Kendall's part of my story, for better or worse."

Hugo pulled on each of my fingers lengthwise. "Why don't you just lie back, Dr. Bloom. You're always thinking and analyzing. Just be still for a bit."

That sounded like a good idea. I relaxed my head into my pillow and closed my eyes, focusing on the warm sensations in my hand. After a few minutes, I started to feel woozy, but not in a bad way. All the pain and suffering melted away.

I felt like my consciousness had detached from my body and I could control its movement. I happily floated out of my body and rose toward the ceiling. Moving to the corner of the room, I looked down to see Hugo still rubbing my hand. I felt the urge to leave the room and explore, so I directed my consciousness down the stairs and out the center's front door. I drifted high into the sky and stared out over the forest. The densely packed trees had started dropping their leaves in preparation for winter.

"Dr. Bloom?"

Hugo's voice brought me out of my daydream, and reality flooded back into my awareness. I couldn't stay blissed-out any longer. I needed to face the problem.

I knew I could put a stop to all of this if I just asked Hugo to call the police. His phone contained all the evidence we needed to incriminate Kendall. But that would lead the authorities to discover our program and undoubtedly shut it down. Plus, turning her into the police would likely mean losing her. I didn't want that.

"We need to take back control of this situation," I said. "Maybe there's a way we could slow her down."

Hugo stopped massaging my hand. "How so?"

"Did I ever tell you how Project Breakthrough began?"

He shook his head.

"Kendall actually started it, not me. I resisted the idea at first."

"Really?"

"She was our first patient," I said, shaking my head in disbelief. "She deliberately ate meat to trigger her allergy."

"Meat?"

"Yeah, some people who've had a tick-borne illness can develop an allergy to meat. When I told her I wouldn't make her sick to spark some creative breakthrough, she ate meatloaf and showed up on my doorstep looking like death."

"Well, that's batshit crazy," Hugo said. "Why tell me this now?"

"Kendall's poisoning me, so why not do the same to her?"

"You want to poison your girlfriend?"

"I just want to slow her down, so we can get back control."

Hugo sat back abruptly.

"Listen," I continued, "there's a container of cooked ground beef in the basement freezer. If you can just get some of it to the kitchen's refrigerator, I'll do the rest."

"How do you expect Kendall to eat something she knows is toxic? And how do you expect to get to the kitchen for that matter?"

I lifted the cane Hugo had brought me.

He folded his arms across his chest. "Look, Dr. Bloom, I'm grateful to you for giving me this job. It's been a wonderful learning opportunity. But I can't do what you're asking. What if she got really sick? What if she died? That'd be murder."

Hugo was right. What was I saying? How had it come to this? Had Project Breakthrough warped my sense of right and wrong? Or maybe I just wanted this suffering to stop so badly, I'd justify anything.

"You're right. It's a terrible idea. Forget I ever mentioned it."

"I should go," Hugo said, standing up. He glanced at the window and bit his lip. "I'm going to close this window. I don't want you to catch a cold."

* * *

In the middle of the night, I was jolted out of sleep by a loud click.

Lifting my head, I tried to figure out where the sound had come from. I wanted to get out of bed and investigate, but I wasn't sure I'd be able to; my legs felt like concrete.

The click sounded again from the direction of the window. Throwing my blanket off, I used my hands to swing my legs off the bed one at a time. When both feet were settled on the floor, I looked at the window, just in time to see something hit the glass. Either a large insect was trying to get in, or someone was hoping to get my attention.

I turned and stared at the cane leaning against the nightstand. Taking a deep breath, I grabbed it and gingerly leaned forward, putting my weight on the wooden pole. With all the strength I could muster, I pushed myself upright and crept forward.

I reached the window a few minutes later, breathless and weak. Gritting my teeth, I opened the window and stuck my head out. Hugo stood in the grass below, a small collection of pebbles in his hand.

"Hugo?" I yelled. "What's going on?"

"Shh! Kendall's in the basement with patients. Talk softly."

I lowered my voice. "Talk about what?"

"I did what you asked me to do."

Relief washed over me in that moment. "What changed your mind?"

"You've done so much for me. It was the least I could do."

"What have I done for you?"

"I've learned so much watching you help our patients. What you offer them can't be measured; it's powerful for those who are suffering."

I asked him what he meant.

Hugo let the pebbles fall. "Most of the doctors I've worked with are obsessed with 'fixing' their patients' problems—with drugs, surgeries, high-tech tools—but sometimes, all a sick person needs is comfort. That's what you taught me, Dr. Bloom, and that's why I'm helping you."

Chapter Twenty-Eight

The next morning, I woke up and immediately wanted to go back to sleep. I was in bad shape. My head pounded and my muscles felt pumped full of acid. Hugo had done his part. Did I have the energy or the courage to do mine? Just getting to the window felt like a herculean effort; how was I supposed to get downstairs and into the kitchen?

And what would I do if I even found a way to get meat into Kendall's body? I could call someone, but I didn't know who. I ruled out the police; should I call Arthur? The patients' families? And what should become of the Breakthrough patients? I'd obviously take them off chemo, but should I continue the program or shut it down? Had we made some kind of beautiful mistake?

Knowing I needed to move, I gritted my teeth and turned toward the bedroom door. Putting most of my weight on the cane, I shuffled across the room. It took five minutes for me to reach the door because every few steps, I had to stop to catch my breath. By the time I opened the door, my heart was pounding. Once I reached the top of the stairs, I put all my weight on the railing and carefully descended to the first floor.

Fifteen minutes later, I was in the kitchen. Once there, I yanked at my sweat-drenched shirt in an attempt to cool down and slumped into a chair at the kitchen table to catch my breath. I pressed my head against the tabletop, feeling completely drained. I couldn't rest long, though. I needed to find a way to get Kendall to ingest meat.

For a couple minutes, I just sat at the table, stumped. I looked around the kitchen, hoping for some inspiration, when my eyes landed on the blender. That's it! Why not blend it into a smoothie? The other ingredients should mask the meat's color and taste. It was a long shot, but it was the only thing my foggy brain could come up with.

Using the cane, I pushed myself upright and hobbled over to the refrigerator. When I opened it, I didn't see the meat. I tried not to panic, reminding myself that if it had been easy to spot, Kendall could've found it. Shifting food around and opening drawers, I finally found the ground beef tucked behind a bag of broccoli in the tray beneath the bottom shelf. It was still partially frozen, but I figured the ice and meat would break up in the blender.

I got to work making a smoothie just the way she liked it: blueberries, strawberries, banana, Greek yogurt, and cinnamon. With some difficulty, I popped the lid off the container of meat and dumped the icy ground beef into the blender.

When I checked on the smoothie's progress, I was glad to see that the brown of the meat was starting to disappear, leaving the whole mix a dark purplish color.

Thinking it was done, I pulled out two mason jars, knowing Kendall would find the whole operation suspicious if I didn't take any for myself. I poured the thick liquid into the two jars, trying not to spill any on the counter.

I threw the beef's storage container into the trash and tucked it under the top layer of garbage to cover my tracks.

I was loading the dishes into the dishwasher when I heard footsteps behind me. I spun around and saw Kendall standing at the edge of the kitchen, squinting at me.

"Cal? What are you doing? How did you even get down here?"

Stepping in front of the trash can, I lifted my cane. "Hugo gave me this."

She frowned. "I see."

Faking a smile, I tried to sound sincere. "I feel like my sickness has driven a wedge between us, Kendall. I miss the us we used to be before I got sick. I thought I'd make smoothies for us—you know, for old times' sake."

She grinned with a suddenness that made me wary. "That's so sweet of you. You make the *best* smoothies." Walking up to me, she squeezed my face. "You're the cutest psychiatrist this side of the Mississippi, you know that?"

I laughed, trying to hide my relief.

Taking one of the jars from me, she looked out the window. "Let's take these out onto the deck, just like we used to do."

I wanted so badly to just lie down and sleep, but I nodded. I reached for my cane, but Kendall took my arm and wrapped it around her shoulder. "I've got you." Bearing my weight, she guided me slowly out onto the deck.

Feeling the chilly breeze on my face, I realized I hadn't been outside in so long. I'd forgotten how refreshing it was to breathe in the fresh air and how pleasing it was to listen to the sounds of the forest: the chirping of crickets, birds flitting between trees, squirrels and other critters scurrying about, the distant hoot of a hidden owl.

We stood at the railing, just enjoying nature's music. For a brief moment, I forgot I was a prisoner in my own home.

In the periphery of my vision, Kendall brought the mason jar to her mouth. Just as she was about to take a sip, though, she lowered it. "You know, Cal, I envy you."

I turned to stare at her, confused.

"It might sound perverse, but you're the sickest patient the Bloom Center's ever had. When you recover, I think you're going to experience something remarkable."

"That's *if* I recover."

"Sure, this is worse than the first time, but I have faith you'll come out better on the other side."

"I'm not so sure I'm going to experience this big breakthrough you think I'm going to have. There's a difference between my situation and our patients', you know."

"How so?"

"Our patients *chose* to come here, get sick, and suffer; I didn't have a choice. I'm suffering against my will. Suffering you choose is different from suffering you don't choose. Plenty of people decide to take part in painful activities that can give them pleasure once they've finished because it lets them escape from consciousness."

"Yeah, like what?"

"Climbing mountains, watching scary movies, running marathons. Cyclists call the pain they experience during long-distance rides 'sweet pain.' Project Breakthrough is *chosen* suffering that gives our patients' lives more meaning. What's happening to me wasn't chosen. I'm afraid my suffering will have no benefit."

Kendall looked pensive. "But what about your writing? There's meaning in recording your experiences, is there not?"

"Writing has helped me cope with my illness, yes, and make sense of some of the other problems here."

She turned to meet my gaze. "What kind of problems?"

I raised my eyebrows. "Oh, I don't know, problems like you taking control of Project Breakthrough and giving patients chemo. Problems like you giving me the same poison that's kept me in bed for weeks. *Those* kinds of problems."

She smiled. "Oh, those. Right."

A long silence followed. Again, I thought Kendall might drink, but she just stared into the jar and then set it on the deck's railing.

"You'd like to stop me, I suppose? Get back at me? All I'm doing is pushing our program to the places it needs to go. I'm pushing *you* where you need to go."

I stared at her, silently begging her to drink from the jar.

"I suppose that's why you spiked my smoothie."

A cold jolt ran through me. I looked away and held my breath.

"Did you really think I wasn't going to watch Hugo closely after he visited you? I knew you two would get up to something, but I never thought you'd try to do something like this."

"Kendall, please. I just want to slow things down. It's too much—"

She picked up the mason jar, reached out over the railing and upended it. I watched as the thick liquid poured from the jar and splashed to the ground below.

Chapter Twenty-Nine

I couldn't have gotten to my room by myself, weak as I was, so Kendall helped me up the stairs. I groaned in pain the whole trip. When we finally reached my bed, I crashed into it, my lungs struggling, head spinning.

Kendall left the room, saying nothing. I shut my eyes. I wanted to pass out and forget about everything—Project Breakthrough, Kendall and her warped ideas, my body's rebellion, which seemed unlikely to ever end.

Light shone through the window when I woke. How long had I slept? I peered at the clock on the wall, which read 4:30 p.m. I'd slept for fourteen hours, but I didn't feel rested. Despite the fatigue, brain fog, back spasms, despite it all, I felt a sudden urge to write. I snatched up my notebook and began scribbling with gusto.

For the rest of the day and all through the night, I wrote and wrote. I wrote a lot about Kendall—about how far she'd gone with our patients, with me, about how dangerous she'd become. Tethered to this bed, without my phone or any way to signal for help, I tried to make sense of this woman I no longer knew, if I ever had, and the actions she'd taken. It was ironic that she'd given me this notebook and now I was wielding it against her. Anyone who read these words would know what she'd done.

After hours of writing, I could barely hold my pen when I heard a knock on the door. Though I didn't respond, the door slowly opened to reveal Kendall. She walked in carrying a large tray, on which sat a glass of wine, a salad bowl, and a plate covered with a silver-domed lid.

She used her foot to close the door behind her. "How's my favorite therapist?"

Setting down my pen, I closed the notebook and just stared at her.

"I thought you'd be hungry after all the writing you've been doing. There's nothing quite as healing as a home-cooked meal."

She rarely cooked. What was she planning? Who was this woman? How had I fallen in love with her?

Kendall placed the tray on the bed.

"So, you know how we always joke about the Bloom Center being a two-star Michelin restaurant? Well, I think I just earned us our third star."

I didn't respond. I wasn't hungry, but I didn't know how she'd react if I said so.

She lifted the domed cover to reveal a plate of baked potatoes, two slices of buttered bread, a side of broccoli, and to my surprise, a large piece of steak.

"What is this?"

"You mean that magnificent piece of porterhouse steak? It was my favorite before I became allergic. Bon appétit!"

I lowered my head in disgust. "I'm not hungry,"

She looked at the steak and sighed. "C'mon, have some. We need to get your weight back up."

"My stomach hurts, Kendall. Food isn't appealing when I'm feeling so—"

"Have some!" she shouted.

I blinked rapidly, then slowly picked up a fork and knife. My hands shook as I cut off a piece of the steak and brought it to my mouth. The meat was juicy, but I could barely look at food, let alone enjoy eating it.

I set the fork and knife down. "It's good." I cleared my throat. "Thank you, but that's all I really have the appetite for right now."

"I see." She pursed her lips. "I'd hate to see such a wonderful dinner go to waste." Grabbing her own fork and knife, she sectioned off a large piece of the steak.

"What are you doing?" I asked.

"I'm not going to throw away a homemade dinner." Bringing the fork to her mouth, she bit into the piece of steak. She chewed and groaned theatrically. "Mmm."

"You're going to get sick."

She closed her eyes and continued chewing.

"Why are you doing this?"

She cut off another piece of steak, put it in her mouth, and chomped loudly. Then she ate another. And another. In between bites, she explained herself. "As I've watched you struggle with your illness, I've realized you're right—I don't think you're going to recover. I think you're going to stay in this bed, or another bed, permanently."

She chewed some more.

"You were never able to show the world the true power of Project Breakthrough. Know why? Because you're too weak. That's why I always have to do what you're too much of a coward to."

I stared at her. "I wish I'd never met you, Kendall."

"Stop being so dramatic, Calvin. Really, what would you have done without me? You think talk therapy's going to solve people's real problems? Of course not! And you knew that. You've always known that. That's why you've needed me every step of the way. To push you to places you're too chickenshit to go."

She swallowed another piece. "So, why am I eating this meat? To make myself sick again—sicker than before—so I can reach a state of consciousness that's out of reach for most people, *including you*. That way, we'll finally see our program's full potential."

"That amount of meat might kill you."

"Hugo let me know how much I could probably get away with."

I felt like I was going to cry.

"Why so blue, dear?"

"Because I'm ashamed of what this center has become! I'm ashamed of who *I've* become, as a man, as a doctor. All I wanted was to help people—heal them—but I'm not a healer. I've hurt people. That's my legacy."

Kendall finished the steak with one final bite. Then she used a napkin to wipe grease from her lips. "I thought you might feel that way," she said, nodding. "That's why I prepared a special dessert for you." Reaching across the tray, she lifted a napkin to reveal a syringe filled with clear liquid.

"What in God's name is that?"

"That, my love, is a full dose of the chemo you've been taking. A lethal dose, actually. If you're so ashamed of yourself and think you'll never recover, why don't you take back control? Do you really want to spend the rest of your life on your back?"

I couldn't deny her logic, morbid as it was. Every day, I seemed to get worse, and I'd probably never return to life as it was before the illness. What kind of life would that be, tethered to a mattress and depending on others to keep me alive?

That wasn't a life I wanted to live. Lying back, I rested my head against the pillow and held out my hand. "Give it to me," I said solemnly.

Without hesitation, Kendall placed the syringe in my palm. Examining it, I broke into tears. How had it come to this? How had I let myself descend back into illness after what happened on my trip? Perhaps I'd flown too close to the sun with Project Breakthrough, but it was Kendall who had pushed me into the flames.

She's right, I thought. I'm weak and afraid. A coward.

Tears rolled down my cheeks as I pulled off the plastic needle cap. I brought the syringe to my left arm. Kendall watched with a bizarre gleam in her eyes.

For some reason, at that moment, the song "Live Like You Were Dying" popped into my mind. The melody ringing in my ears, I thought of Chase and Annette, who'd discovered new identities in Project Breakthrough, who'd decided to spend their lives together. It made me happy to have helped them and the others. I thought of Max and hoped he was okay. If I could somehow get out of this mess, I could help more people.

I placed the syringe on the tray. "I can't do it."

Kendall exhaled. "You know, there's something I never told you when I was in therapy. Something I've hidden from you all this time."

I wiped tears from my eyes. "What's that?"

"It's about my dad. I told you about how weak I thought he was. How he didn't have the guts to figure out who he was and what he wanted out of life. I told you he'd gotten sick and died. But I never told you how."

I paused, recalling our therapy sessions. "You said he died of a heart attack."

"He did, but that's not the whole story. About a month before I met you, I was at my dad's house for dinner when that big fat heart of his finally started giving out at the kitchen table. He gripped his chest saying it felt like there was a tractor on his chest. He screamed at me to call an ambulance. Know what I did?"

I raised my eyebrows, waiting for an answer.

"Absolutely *nothing*. I just sat there and watched him die. He'd done nothing with his pathetic life. Why save him? All he did was take and take, giving or creating nothing. He was a drag on the economy, a drag on our family, a complete waste of space. I didn't call an ambulance until after he was gone. He died right there at the table, his face buried in his plate of pasta."

I stared at her. "Why would you tell me that awful story now?"

Her face twisted into a glare. "Because that's how I feel about you, Cal.

I'm more disappointed by you than my dad. Know why? Because you have potential, but you lack the ambition, the imagination, to take our project to the next level."

She snatched the syringe from the tray.

I recoiled and pressed my back against the headboard. "W-what are you doing?"

"I didn't kill my dad, Cal, I just didn't save him."

I held up my hands in desperation. "Please . . . don't—"

In one swift motion, she plunged the needle into my thigh. I jerked my leg away, but it didn't matter. She'd emptied the contents into my body.

"You bitch!" I screamed. "What have you done?"

"I did what you couldn't, as usual."

I thought about the drug's properties. How long before it overwhelmed my system and killed me? Fifteen minutes? Less?

Replacing the needle cap, Kendall set the empty syringe on the tray, and moved it to the floor. Kicking off her shoes, she lifted the blanket, slid in beside me, and pressed her body against mine. Under the blanket, she grabbed my hand and interlocked our fingers.

"Kind of romantic, if you ask me," she whispered. "Two lovers make themselves sick in pursuit of a breakthrough in consciousness."

My eyes flitted back and forth as I searched for an answer. What could I do? I might've been able to call to a patient, but I didn't want to call for help.

Unexpectedly, I heard Arthur's words echo in my mind—"Never waste an illness"—and I had the strange desire to finish what I'd started.

"Kendall?"

Her tone was unexpectedly sweet. "Yes, dear?"

"Can you hand me my notebook, please?"

Smiling, she put the notebook on my lap and the pen in my hand.

After Dr. Bloom's passing, I felt someone should tell the rest of his story and help carry it into the world. That person, as it turned out, was me: Dr. Arthur Pratt. Since you just finished this book, I assume I need no introduction.

I'm sure you have many questions: What happened after Dr. Bloom died? Did Kendall pass away too? If so, what became of the Bloom Center? Project Breakthrough? Perhaps you're curious about what happened to me. In these last few pages, I hope to address all your questions.

I'll begin where Dr. Bloom's story left off.

On the night Dr. Bloom left us, I woke in the middle of the night to his nurse knocking on my door. Breathless and scared, Hugo told me he thought something awful was going to happen soon. We decided to drive to the center that night.

When Hugo and I arrived around three in the morning, the building was eerily quiet.

"Dr. Bloom!" I shouted from the lobby.

No answer.

"Kendall?" Hugo called out.

Nothing.

We climbed the stairs to Dr. Bloom's room, afraid of what we might find. Nothing prepared me for the sight that greeted us. When I opened the door, I covered my mouth in horror. There, lying in bed, were Dr. Bloom and Kendall, still as statues.

I told Hugo to call the police. As he reported the incident, I moved closer to the bed. I removed the blanket and saw that Dr. Bloom and Kendall were holding hands. In his right hand, Dr. Bloom was holding a pen, its tip pressed to the page of the notebook I'd seen when I last visited him. Prying the notebook from beneath his hand, I scanned the pages. It didn't take me long to realize just what Dr. Bloom had written.

Ten minutes later, police cars filled the driveway, and an ambulance arrived to pick up the bodies. After giving a statement to the detectives, I walked out onto the center's back deck and stared into the woods for several minutes, staggered by what had happened. Realizing Project Breakthrough had to be disbanded immediately, I asked Hugo to call the patients' families and inform them that I'd stay at the center long enough to help wean the patients off their drugs.

For the next few hours, I sat on the deck and finished reading Dr. Bloom's book. At first, I was touched by this well-written memoir about a psychiatrist who tried to help the most challenging patients, only to lose his way. Then I grew horrified as I read about Kendall's influence on my friend, placing herself and others in more and more danger in search of an unattainable ideal.

Setting the book down, I realized that Dr. Bloom had finally written something he was proud of. Sure, it sometimes read like a manifesto, but his memoir felt more like an ethical inquiry than a statement that illness transforms everyone. I knew I needed to help get this book out into the world for others to read.

It's only right that Dr. Bloom has the last words. Apparently, as he lay dying, he chose to finish his story, confessing that it was the only courageous thing he'd ever done.

> *As I write this, my hands shake, my eyelids feel heavy. All I want is to pass out, slip away. I've spent many days afraid of dying, but I no longer feel scared. I wrote a story worth telling, and hope others can find lessons in it.*

One thing I've learned in my work with patients, and in our program, is that life isn't supposed to be easy—adversity can teach us the most important lessons.

In that vein, I end my story with the following: Through pain and suffering, we learn empathy and compassion. Through betrayal, we understand loyalty. By being treated unfairly, we understand justice.

Suffering does make us stronger, and I hope my story gives you the strength you need.

THE END

Selected Bibliography for Further Reading

Anatomy of an Illness: As Perceived by the Patient by Norman Cousins

Molecules of Emotion: The Science Behind Mind-Body Medicine by Candace Pert

Healing Back Pain by John Sarno

Being Mortal: Medicine and What Matters in the End by Atul Gawande

The Man Who Mistook His Wife for a Hat by Oliver Sacks

When Breath Becomes Air by Paul Kalanithi

A Fortunate Man: The Story of a Country Doctor by John Berger

A Thousand-Mile Walk to the Gulf by John Muir

Closing the Chart: A Dying Physician Examines Family, Faith, and Medicine by Steven D. Hsi

The Invisible Kingdom: Reimagining Chronic Illness by Meghan O'Rourke

The Lady's Handbook for Her Mysterious Illness: A Memoir by Sarah Ramey

9 798999 268870